T0014132

# YESTERDAYS

HAROLD SONNY LADOO

foreword by
KEVIN JARED HOSEIN

Coach House Books, Toronto

Copyright © The Estate of Harold Sonny Ladoo, 1974, 2024
Foreword copyright © Kevin Jared Hosein, 2024
First published in 1974 by House of Anansi Press

Published with the generous assistance of the Canada Council for the Arts and the Ontario Arts Council.

LIBRARY AND ARCHIVES CANADA CATALOGUING IN PUBLICATION

Title: Yesterdays / Harold Sonny Ladoo ; foreword by Kevin Jared Hosein.
Names: Ladoo, Harold Sonny, 1945- author. | Hosein, Kevin Jared, writer of foreword.
Description: Previously published: Toronto: Anansi, 1974.
Identifiers: Canadiana (print) 20240364899 | Canadiana (ebook) 2024036497X | ISBN 9781552454787 (softcover) | ISBN 9781770568020 (PDF) | ISBN 9781770568013 (EPUB)
Subjects: LCGFT: Novels.
Classification: LCC PS8573.A28 Y3 2024 | DDC 813 | C813/.54—dc23

Yesterdays is available as an ebook: ISBN 978 1 77056 801 3 (EPUB), 978 1 77056 802 0 (PDF)

Purchase of the print version of this book entitles you to a free digital copy. To claim your ebook of this title, please email sales@chbooks.com with proof of purchase. (Coach House Books reserves the right to terminate the free digital download offer at any time.)

# FOREWORD
## by Kevin Jared Hosein

*Equal to Mystery*, Christopher Laird's biography of Harold Sonny Ladoo, contains a striking letter from Ladoo to his editor. The novelist reveals endearing honesty as he laments the lack of tragedy in his life, at least in comparison to his characters' lives. A statement that would take on a different hue shortly after, in 1973, upon his murder, unsolved to this day. And his death, as unfortunate and enigmatic as it was, would lend a grim surreality to the two books he gave to the world.

For much of my teenage and young adult reading life, my tastes skewed toward the dark, the profane, the dystopian. From the lonesome barflies in Bukowski's poetry to the blood-red border landscapes of Cormac McCarthy and the dreamlike psychopathy of David Lynch's films. There was always something deeply moving about wandering through the tragedies of these invented worlds. And I had always wanted to find a Caribbean novel like that: one that not only exposed the violence of our society, but subverted it, revelled in it. For too long – the entirety of my primary and secondary school days – I regarded Caribbean literature as solely reading and comprehension exercises, safe and sanitary enough for the school textbook shelf.

It was only when I encountered Ladoo's *No Pain Like This Body*, his debut, that I realized Caribbean literature could be as deliciously discourteous and wayward as the American works that had so captivated me. In that book, set in a rice-farming community in 1905 Trinidad, the horrid and the violent are portrayed as commonplace. Many characters seem affectless and there is almost no respite from suffering, for anything alive. This debut, which is now over fifty years old, opened a door and beckoned for me to reconsider Caribbean literature – to look beyond the more wholesome, secondary-school-friendly books I had been exposed to. Ugliness is a necessity for any artform.

Ladoo was born and raised in central Trinidad. As was I. Living in a simultaneously small island community and a big family can drive any writer to pen only safe and sophisticated stories, stories that will please the church, the mandir, the mosque, the aunties, the family lime. After all, those closest to you are often the first people you want to accept your work. And for many writers in countries that lack the muscle of a traditional publishing industry, your community and family are probably going to serve as your entire marketing department and customer base – though not so much your readership, as family and neighbours tend to buy books but never read them. Probably for the best. Marlon James knows this; his dedication in his own debut, *John Crow's Devil*, reads: 'To my mother, who must not read this book.'

And it was on a panel about Laird's biography of Ladoo at the Bocas Literature Festival that I learned of the divided opinions on *Yesterdays*. That it is a book probably best not read. Ladoo's publisher had initially rejected the manuscript. At my panel, Jeremy Poynting of Peepal Tree Press, one of the most prominent champions of Caribbean literature, hesitated when the idea came up of bringing *Yesterdays* back into the world. To let it out on parole. When I asked a respected literary colleague about the book, he squirmed, his expression souring as if he had just sipped spoiled milk. In my mind, it was like that one line from Tarantino's *Django Unchained*:

*It had my curiosity … but now it had my attention.*

In letters to his editor, Ladoo fiercely defended his manuscript and was adamant about its structure and style. He implied that *Yesterdays* would be a bridge, or perhaps even a narrow stairway, to something epic, something opus-like. That *Yesterdays* would be a sort of literary liminal space. He claimed to have been working on several additional manuscripts and that *Yesterdays* was a necessary brushstroke for his grand portrait of the indentured. Something about the letters, the cunningness and desperation in his words, came across to me like the plea of a Trinidadian schemer-man.

He had, after all, claimed to have grown up in an orphanage despite both his parents being alive and well. This to his Canadian mentor, an actual orphan. The scar on his neck – was it from a knife fight, or a reckless brush with his father's cutlass? To Ladoo, each version could be right, depending on whom he was telling. Right, in this case, being different from true. Truth, after all, has no versions. Perhaps Ladoo had accepted the archetype of male writers having to posture as warriors in order to prosper, to be apotheosized and canonized – Hemingway donning boxing gloves, Mishima in his headband with a swordsman's stance, Orwell's bloody mouth after a sniper's bullet pierced his throat.

In Ladoo's time, and the time of so many others, a person anchored on these Caribbean rocks, becoming a writer did require a warrior's essence. It still does, today. To wish to write was to uproot oneself and stand naked in the oppressive British and Canadian cold in the hope of writing to an audience about everything unfamiliar to them. Our Creole words and mechanisms of grammatical expression, which can pad out any novel if fully glossarized. The idiosyncracies of our villages' cultural customs. That Caribbean grief is its own thing, and the sinister humour that accompanies that grief – laugh and cry does live in the same house.

And if *No Pain Like This Body* was cry, Ladoo meant for *Yesterdays* to be laugh. And humour, unlike sorrow, can be highly subjective. Trinidadian humour can be very dark, but *Yesterdays* takes that humour through catacomb depths. Even my own morbid sensibilities were shaken by this book, which is less of laugh than a madman cackling at your neighbour's exploded outhouse. Upon the first read, *Yesterdays* made me feel dirty, but also something I hadn't truly experienced before with Caribbean literature –

I was offended.

In one scene, under the guidance of a corrupt, cowboy-boot-wearing Saddhu who denounces indoor sex, a married couple copulates outside their house and becomes stuck like post-coital dogs, much to the amusement of the entire village. In another scene, a character scratches his balls while declaring, *Hitler could kiss me ass!* Sook – lech first, then a shopkeeper – manages to seduce most of the novel's male cast. When a character is thought to be dead, he bemoans not the character's death but the missed opportunity to penetrate them. Choonilal, our protagonist, opts to use latrines despite having a commode installed in his house. This because he believes it sinful to pass bowel movements at home. Basically, another version of not shitting where you eat. His lodger, Tailor, has left the latrine in a nauseating state, which prompts Choonilal to negotiate with neighbours for the use of their latrines. This happens numerous times in this fairly short book, as if Choonilal's bowel movements are a Pavlovian response to his mounting stresses. This also prompts Choonilal's wife, Basdai, to empty her bowels in the adjacent canefield.

My own ancestors would have grown up in a rural community similar to the one Ladoo describes. They may have engaged in such antics, but everything here seemed so greatly exaggerated. I asked myself if Ladoo wanted his audience to point their fingers and laugh at these villagers. If he had created them with the sole intention of degrading them. I asked myself: why would he turn the Hindu Indo-Trinidadian community into such a farce?

Then my mind reeled to a video I had seen of an audience Q&A at the Cannes Film Festival. It was for a film called *Better Luck Tomorrow*, about a group of Asian-American students committing an escalating series of crimes. An audience member asked the director, and I paraphrase: Why would you make a film so amoral? Why would you represent Asian Americans this way? To which the famed critic Roger Ebert sprung up and exclaimed, 'This film has the right to be about these people, and Asian Americans have the right to be whatever the hell they want to be. They do not have to "represent" their people.'

This was important for me to remember.

And I think it may be a trap when writers feel they must represent themselves in a realist way.

*Yesterdays* is not realist. In fact, it may be – and I know the term is overused – postmodernist.

And so I re-read the book, focusing this time on the parts with Poonwa, the highly educated and ambitious son of Choonilal and Basdai. Poonwa wishes for his father to mortgage the house to fund his trip to Canada to create what might be described as a Hindu

Schutzstaffel, starting by establishing a school with a torture chamber. A revenge plot ignited by his Canadian missionary schoolteacher who abusively coaxed Poonwa's Hindu classmates to convert to Christianity. He had punished her in his mind over a thousand times. But it was not enough. He would have to end Christianity. Poonwa speaks in stilted standard English, almost to a comedic fault, often referencing alien figures such as Nietzsche and Galileo and Marx. Perhaps this was Ladoo's vision of the warrior-as-writer: a raider of foreign literary landscapes, preaching principles that they themselves have not obeyed. After all, Poonwa wants to export Hinduism to Canada while being unable to speak any Hindi. Perhaps Poonwa's mental state was Ladoo's warning to himself.

*Yesterdays* is a slice of filthy life. Ladoo built a world and a fractured reality where a fly-haloed latrine is used as currency. As leverage. As a haven for a child. In this world, wives are flogged in the village street. Gynecologists regularly molest their patients. A villager's keepsake is an American rapist's towel. A Hindu pundit licks his lips while staring at a woman's labia. All while the white men in Canada sip whisky and dream in peace. It is not an aesthetic that can be easily appreciated. But Ladoo managed to write something that dug deep into colonial trauma. It is not a perfect novel – or even a great one, thanks to its clunky first act and treatment of the queer shopkeeper in its narration – but it is one that struck my nerve endings. And I hope more books are written in this vein. And I hope even more that they are read.

## A Note from the Publisher

*Yesterdays* is an unfinished book. Harold Sonny Ladoo was murdered, in 1973, before editing was completed. It is a big departure from his first book, *No Pain Like This Body*, and it shows a trajectory to his writing career that might have changed the course of Canadian literature.

The coarse scenarios and vocabulary Ladoo used may have been an attempt to distract from the rage simmering beneath, or they may have been an attempt to shock a staid CanLit. Whatever the motivation, there is much in this book to offend the reader.

We opted not to temper the dated and insensitive vocabulary or tame the objectionable scenes; we've cleaned up a few typographical errors and rogue punctuation, but otherwise left the text as is. This edition of *Yesterdays* is an effort to preserve history and to allow us to imagine how Ladoo might have reconfigured our literature had he lived.

*Rachel*

*Walter Dmytrenko & Florence Murray & Sylvia Sookram*
*Jeofferey Saigal & Durani Vidyapati & Linda Wbber & Lawrence J. Elmer & Josef*
*Skvorecky & Shirley G.*

*Jim Polk*

KARAN SETTLEMENT
MARCH 1955

Tailor sat under the chataigne tree; with a worried face he counted the cars as they passed by. With old embroidery scissors, he picked his teeth.

Choonilal sat on an old potato crate a few feet away from Tailor and brushed his teeth with a guava stick. Occasionally he glanced at Tailor with a worried face. As Tailor's landlord he was obviously displeased about something, and he was thinking something bad too: there was a strangeness in his glance as if he were secretly planning to murder his tenant.

There was a Jandee pole in the yard; every good Hindu in Karan Settlement had a pole like it. The pole reminded them that life only called upon a greater life, that a higher form of being after death was what life was all about, and that the Aryan gods lived around the Jandee pole – not only lived but gazed upon their activities, and not gazed alone but recorded all that they did, recorded their deeds not in some eternal book in some faraway region but in their own hearts; and they, whether they wanted their hearts to keep records of their activities or not, could do nothing to prevent the recording, for the Aryan gods were not in the habit of consulting man; they just willed his own heart to keep the records and willed the heart to keep true records; these same records that man was willed to keep were the same records that were going to release him from the unending cycle of life and death or doom him to suffer forever.

Choonilal in particular was a good Hindu. In order to keep the records of his heart straight, every morning Choonilal used to offer water to the sun by the Jandee pole, because the Aryan gods lived around the pole. And at times Choonilal wept as he offered water to the Aryan gods in his brass lota; he did this because he felt that the gods were going to recognize the weeping Choonilal after death; this was important, because at times Choonilal had an uneasy feeling. Just last night he had dreamt that he was dead and the records of his heart proved that he had done more evil than good. This dream bothered Choonilal as he brushed his teeth. For two months now he hadn't offered a single drop of water to the gods. This was because of the war that waged in his household. He knew that the gods were waiting for the water, but he thought it best to neglect them until his domestic affairs were settled. Choonilal knew that quarrelling and fighting were not good things. These activities were going to make him born as a snake or a worm after death. He brooded a little and remembered that even the gods waged war to establish righteousness; this gave him strength to keep on quarrelling with Tailor. Once Choonilal had warned Tailor. That was the time when Tailor had threatened to bite out Basdai's nose. But in those days Tailor was a different person.

Choonilal brushed his teeth slowly. At times he glanced at the Jandee pole from which hung a red flag. It was as if Choonilal was studying the impressive figure of the Hindu god Hanuman. Hanuman was painted in white – painted in such a skilful way that Tailor thought the monkey god used to talk to his landlord. At first Choonilal liked the idea of the god talking to him (a rumour started by Tailor), but when Choonilal found out Tailor had told people that Hanuman used to insult him and call him an evil man, Choonilal decided to put a stop to Tailor. Choonilal was proud of the Jandee pole and proud of Hanuman. Hanuman is the God of Power, and Choonilal wanted power.

'Nearly two years you livin by me, Tailor!'

'Look, Choonilal, you coud kiss me royal ass!' Tailor said.

'Who de hell you bawlin at? Look boy, watch you mout. Oright! Two years you livin by me. Two kiss-me-ass years! You never pay a cent rent. You never pay for food. You rotten ting, you!'

'Look Choonilal, I not livin by you two years! It is nearly two years, but not two years. Too besides you is not me fadder, Choonilal. You hear dat!'

And Choonilal: 'Two years you livin by me. Two kiss-me-ass years! But you better pay dat rent you owe. Den clean dat latrine. You hear dat?'

'Like someting worryin you, old-ass Choonilal? Well, lemme tell you someting. I not payin no rent! I not cleanin dat latrine eidder!'

'Tailor!'

'Yeh!'

'You does shit de most in dat latrine. You is de man who does leggo fat fat leer in it. Den you have to clean it.'

'Kiss me ass!' Tailor shouted.

And Choonilal: 'Tailor, I is a religious man! A kiss-me-ass religious man! You hear dat? But wen you dead you go born back a blasted worm in a latrine. Oright!'

Tailor threw away the embroidery scissors. Standing upright, he said to Choonilal, 'You givin you mout too much liberty, Choonilal! You is not me fadder, you know, Choonilal. So try and hush dat mout of yours.'

All his life Choonilal had been a coward man, yet he was prepared to attack Tailor this morning. So without moving from the potato crate, he continued to insult Tailor, to insult him and tell him all kind of things: things like how he had taken him as a tenant but never collected any rent, things like how Tailor was not born in Karan Settlement, he just came as a dog into the settlement and it was Choonilal who had taken him into his house. He mentioned the fact that he gave Tailor money to go into the sewing business, money Tailor was never grateful enough to repay. When Tailor first came to Karan Settlement, he was thin as a whip; he hadn't enough life even to look for anything to do. Choonilal made his wife, Basdai, cook and wash for Tailor. The Choonilals never took money from him. In those days Tailor never wanted to fight Choonilal. Choonilal accepted him as a son; he gave him the authority to eat, sleep, and empty his bowels in the outhouse any time he liked. In those days Tailor pretended to be a man of God; this was the reason why Choonilal had adopted him in the first place. Every morning Tailor used to wake before sunrise, empty his bowels, and offer water to Hanuman by the Jandee pole. Whenever he wanted to urinate, he used to leave the house and go far into the bushes. In those days the Choonilals loved him.

One morning when Choonilal saw Tailor's devotion to the Aryan gods, he was so moved that he wept; and not only wept alone, he took a taxi and went to Tolaville and bought a nice cot for Tailor to sleep upon. And on another day Tailor had prayed so much that Choonilal went and bought him a new sewing machine. But as time passed by, Tailor never bothered with the gods any more. This offended Choonilal. Not only had Tailor abandoned the gods; he had lost his shame as well. For example, he was in the habit of standing on his landlord's steps and urinating in broad daylight. Then he began to practise sodomy with the village queer. Nights upon nights Tailor used to seduce Sook the village queer downstairs. The queer was in the habit of screaming and getting on so vulgarly that Choonilal couldn't sleep. These activities worried Choonilal, because he was fifty-five years old. He knew that the Aryan gods were going to hold him responsible for Tailor's activities.

As these things flashed through his mind, Choonilal chewed the guava stick with a kind of vengeance. Tailor's sexual appetite was enormous; failing to find sufficient pleasure with the queer, he had picked up a new and expensive habit: he would take Choonilal's money and go to South City and bring whores up to Karan Settlement. All night there used to be drinking, singing, and screwing in Tailor's room downstairs. One night about two months ago, Phyllis, the daughter of Leeza, took a band of whores and came to Karan Settlement. Tailor received them inside his room. That whole night Tailor was screwing this one and that one, and the women were drunk and running all over Choonilal's property. Some of the women were so drunk that they defecated in the yard by the Jandee pole. Phyllis had tried to use Choonilal's outhouse, but she was too drunk to use it carefully. She had emptied her bowels on the floor and knocked down the eastern tapia wall.

'Tailor!' Choonilal screamed.

'Wot de hell you want?'

'Clean dat latrine! You bring people to shit in it, well you have to clean it.'

Tailor didn't say anything. The accusations were true. But those things had happened about two months ago; Choonilal had already forgiven him. Tailor knew exactly what was bothering Choonilal: his son Poonwa wanted five thousand dollars to go to Canada on a Hindu Mission. Choonilal didn't have the money to send his son overseas. Pandit Puru, the village priest, was willing to lend the money to Choonilal, but he was scared to do any business with the priest, because it was known throughout Carib Island that Pandit Puru was a fraud.

'Why you dont say wot really worryin you,' Tailor said. 'You know dat I not doin you one ting.'

'Notten not worryin me! You hear dat? You just try and pay dat rent for de time you live by me. Pay for sleepin, for cookin you food and for washin you cloes. Oright!' Choonilal stood up and, pointing a finger at his tenant, he continued, 'And clean dat latrine. And pay me dat money you owe me for dat sewin machine. Pay me for dat cot you sleepin on. Oright!'

'Well, Choonilal, I tellin you to you face. I not payin no rent! Why you dont give Poon de money and stop you mind from worryin you! And you have to clean dat latrine yourself.'

Choonilal was outraged.

'If I didnt believe in God, Tailor, I wouda hit you one lash and kill you.'

Cars were still passing in the new road. Sook, the village queer, sat in his shop and looked on. He didn't like how Choonilal was getting on with Tailor; he wanted to run out of his shop and insult Choonilal, because he knew that Choonilal was getting on, and getting on not because of the latrine: he was really getting on because he wouldn't get the money to send Poonwa on the Hindu Mission to Canada. But it was very hard for Sook to insult any one of them. He loved Tailor and he loved his neighbour Choonilal also. But it was Sook's business to be up to date in the scandalous affairs of the village; as a queer he had to be informed always. Sook summed up the situation. Choonilal was wrong; he had no right to use the outhouse and the rent and the sewing machine as a front to hide his deeper problems. Sook felt that Choonilal was backing down to Poonwa. But Sook knew that Choonilal and Tailor were not going to fight; they were too coward to have a scuffle. Then it dawned upon Sook that Choonilal might evict Tailor. This discovery made his heart beat faster. Just last night Tailor was in his shop; just last night he had lured Tailor into a homosexual affair. Without Tailor in Karan Settlement, Sook would have to go manhunting again, and manhunting was a lot of trouble in Tola.

Choonilal had a bald head: the reward for those who toil bare-headed in the tropics. But as he stood on the yard and quarrelled with his tenant, he forgot that he had no hair. Now and then he brushed one hand over his reddish skull in an attempt to push back his hair. Thinking about his son's Hindu Mission to Canada, Choonilal got more mad. With one hand kneading his balls and the other scratching his head, he walked up and down in the yard.

'Tailor, pay de money!'

'Like you take a walkin ticket?' Tailor said.

'I take you modder!'

'You cant take me modder, Choonilal! Me modder done rotten in she grave. Watch you blasted mout how you talkin!'

'But it is you who bring dem jamet and dem, and make dem full up de kiss-me-ass pit. But Tailor, it have a God. He watchin you, you know, Tailor.'

'Look, behave, you old-ass, nuh man. You know dat you talkin because Poonwa want money from you. He want de money to go to Canada. Give de kiss-me-ass boy de money. If you dont have it, den tell Poonwa to haul he ass. Act like a big man, Choonilal!'

Choonilal stopped to think. When he had approached the priest two months ago for the money, he told Choonilal that he would give him the money only if he mortgaged his house and land. Choonilal had called off the deal. But for the past two months Choonilal couldn't rest properly; he was so worried that he couldn't even make his mind calm enough to throw water for the sun by the Jandee pole. His son Poonwa kept threatening him every night.

Thinking again about his son's Hindu Mission to Canada, Choonilal complained about the outhouse. He said he couldn't sleep at night because of the terrible stench that came from the pit; when he did get a few minutes' sleep, he always dreamt of excreta and worms. Last night he had dreamt that the Aryan gods came to visit his house, but they couldn't even come close to it. The stench that came from the pit made the gods angry. One of the gods had threatened to doom Choonilal so that for another million years he would be born a worm. This dream made Choonilal scream so much that his wife thought he was dying. As a religious man, Choonilal knew he couldn't take it much longer. If the pit was not cleaned up quickly, he was going to lose the blessings of the gods.

'Tailor!'

'Yeh!'

'Take you lock, stock, and barrel and get outta here!'

Tailor was shocked. Choonilal had always been a good landlord; he was really more than a good landlord; he was a sort of inspiration to Tailor. When he came to Karan Settlement he came as a stranger; he didn't even have an extra suit of clothes; in the book he had names and addresses of the various people he had lived by in different villages. Choonilal had met him in the road, and when he heard that Tailor was a stranger in the village, he took him into his house. He gave Tailor the extra room downstairs and told him to live there. It was some weeks later that Choonilal had enough courage to come around to the embarrassing subject of occupation. Tailor, wishing to create a good impression, said that he had been a tailor from childhood. For Choonilal this was a great achievement; sewing was a great profession, because most of the young men in Karan Settlement were labourers in the sugar estates. Filled with admiration, Choonilal went and bought a sewing machine for Tailor. But Tailor needed more money. He wanted an electric machine. Choonilal wanted to know why he wanted an electric machine. Tailor took his time and gave the reasons to his landlord. Choonilal was fascinated. Tailor made Choonilal take back the hand-operated machine, advising him to get an electric one. So, armed with a good machine, Tailor went headlong into the sewing business. His first jobs were disasters in which Choonilal acted as his saviour. Once he sewed some trousers for a man in China Road. The man took the pants and went away but that same night the man invaded Tailor's little room; he had the trousers in one hand and a blade in the other. Tailor was cornered, so he called on Choonilal and the Aryan gods at the same time. Choonilal ran downstairs, and when he saw the man inside Tailor's room, he called on Sook and Ragbir and the Aryan gods. The man, unable to face Tailor's allies, bolted away. But in spite of the trials and disappointments, tailoring continued to fascinate Choonilal. Choonilal used to spend hours and hours just listening to the sound of the machine; once he was so carried away he told his tenant that by listening to the purring of the machine alone, a man could gain immortality; Tailor had agreed to this of course. Choonilal used to watch the needle as it came down with unbelievable swiftness and stabbed the cloth. It always puzzled him how white people could have made something like a machine.

Once he had asked Tailor how the sewing machine came into being. Tailor made use of the little knowledge he had picked up here and there. He told Choonilal about England and the Industrial Revolution. His landlord took out his eyes big big when he heard about the greatness of England. He had thought all his life that white people knew only about slavery and sugarcane production. Without asking another question, Choonilal began to weep. This had terrified Tailor, because he was a stranger in the village. He asked Choonilal why he was weeping; he said that he was crying because he wanted to go to England. In order to beat the idea out of Choonilal, Tailor told him that white people in England didn't like to bathe because the weather was so cold; they didn't like to brush their teeth either, they believed that chewing gum was better than labouring with a toothbrush; when they emptied their bowels, they wiped their arse with paper. Choonilal was appalled when he got this information. He gave up the idea of going to England. But Choonilal still didn't lose interest in matters pertaining to sewing. He had a capacity for worry. Over a thousand times he asked Tailor why the small wheel in the machine spun, and over a thousand times Tailor furnished him with an answer. After the machine fever had passed, Choonilal developed other kinds of illnesses; he started worrying about why airplanes fly and ships travel on water, why submarines travel underwater and electricity runs along cable wires. For every question, Tailor had an answer, and Choonilal never turned sceptical. This worried Tailor a lot.

'Look Choonilal,' Tailor said, 'tink about de long time we live togedder in Karan Settlement. Remember dem days, man. If you still want to put me outta de house, you can't do dat widdout Basdai agreein for me to leave. Take care wot you doin, Choonilal, because accordin to English Law Basdai have a lotta rights in de house you know.'

'Look Tailor, dont bring me wife in dis talk. Oright!'

'But you couda bring me modder in de talk?'

'If I wasnt a man of God, I wouda done wring out you stones aready. You makin joke wid me, Tailor. Me name is Choonilal you know!'

'You old bitch you! You dont see dat you wife gone Tolaville to take man. She leave you home like a old ass, and she gone to take she man and dem. You stupid ass you. Just now horn goin to grow on you bald head. You dont see you too old now for woman?'

And Choonilal: 'Tailor, old as I is I does still ride me wife you know. She gone Tolaville to buy goods. You sayin she gone to take man. But wen Basdai come back home, you go have to tell she wot you tellin me. Oright!'

And Tailor: 'You cant fool me, Choonilal! You coud never fool me. Your totey cant stand up. If you totey stand up, I drop dead right in dis yard of yours. You dont see dat Basdai have too much backside for you?'

'Look here, Tailor, I does pray to God you know.'

'Dat have notten do to do wid you totey!'

'You tink me totey cant stand up, eh? Well, lemme tell you someting. Just call out to Sook in dat shop! Ask him if me Choonilal's totey never stand up.'

Suddenly Sook shouted out from across the road: 'Ay, Choonilal, watch you kiss me ass mout yeh! Wen I want man, I coud find me own man. Dont try to make no scandal on me name. Too besides, if I does take man, I does take man in me own bumsee. You dont take me man for me you know, Choonilal! It take a able man to take man. Oright.'

Choonilal didn't want to carry on a quarrel on two fronts at the same time. Instead of taking on Sook, he began to complain again about Tailor. According to him it was impossible to use the outhouse by night; to use it by day was unthinkable! One night Choonilal's wife had tried to use the pit, but the light of a passing car flashed upon her and revealed her person in an obscene posture. It was late and there were no pedestrians on the road. Desire rose in the taxidriver when he saw Basdai by the outhouse. He parked the taxi near the bushes and came near her. He waited under the chataigne tree until Basdai was finished. Then he ran out of the dark and dragged her into the canal. Holding her mouth, he climbed on top of her. But Basdai bit his fingers and she started to bawl. When the taxidriver heard her getting on, he pulled up his pants and ran. That night Choonilal took a cutlass and ran out of the house. He made so much noise that his neighbours came to inquire what had happened. When they learnt of Basdai and the taxidriver, instead of helping Choonilal find the lecherous man, they began laughing.

Basdai was a woman of God. After the incident she became so embarrassed that she developed a fever and stayed in Tolaville Hospital for two weeks. She did this to combat the village scandal. When she came out of the hospital, she sent her husband to call Pandit Puru. The priest came and told her that it was not a taxidriver who had raped her; it was an evil spirit. She believed him. The priest took one hundred dollars from her and made her swear that she would never use the outhouse again. Collecting her willpower, Basdai swore on the Hindu Bible that she would never go inside one. Every night after she took the oath, she used to wake at midnight, take the little track at the back of the house, and empty her bowels in the sugarcane field. She felt safe: no one was able to see her in her toilet. But after a week or so, Mrs. Choonilal began to have guilt feelings. She felt that the Aryan gods were going to be mad with her. One night she dreamt that the monkey god Hanuman was running her all over the village. She woke up trembling. Then she sent Choonilal to call the village priest. When Pandit Puru came, he listened to her story. He took some more money from Basdai and told her not to fear. According to the priest, the Aryan gods had great compassion and unlimited knowledge; they knew that Basdai couldn't use the outhouse; once the gods understood her dilemma, she had nothing to worry about.

Choonilal was in no better position. He wanted to use the sugarcane field with his wife, but he couldn't. He was afraid of the dark. Besides that, he used to empty his bowels during the day. Though he had no special hour to shit, he enjoyed an early morning shit better. At times his bowels had their own way. Since the whores had damaged his property, Choonilal was in the habit of defecating in Ragbir's outhouse. Ragbir was Choonilal's eastern neighbour. But in order to get at Ragbir's pit, Choonilal had to cross over the new road. This was a dangerous thing. The cars used to pass through the village at great speeds. On

Sook's Junction alone, twenty people had been killed on one spot within fifteen years.

Choonilal was not always master of his bowel movements. Sometimes he used to run across the road without even bothering to see if the way was clear or not. Just yesterday he had almost been killed. He was offering prayers to the gods while he sat on his front steps, then he felt that he had to defecate right away. He ran out on the junction with one hand massaging his belly and the other squeezing his hips. He saw a line of vehicles travelling in opposite directions. He decided to wait. But suddenly he felt as if all his inner organs were going to fall through his asshole. He screamed and dashed across the road. If the taxidriver had not put on his brakes, he would have died on the spot.

As a religious man, Choonilal had to give thanks every day to the gods for using Ragbir's pit. He knew that Ragbir was going to receive blessings from the gods. Choonilal didn't particularly like the idea. He felt that Ragbir was an evil man; he deserved to be reincarnated as a worm or a snake. But if Choonilal continued to give thanks for using the pit, then Ragbir wouldn't be reborn as a worm or a snake. This worried Choonilal so much that he told Tailor:

'Tailor, I is a kiss-me-ass man of God! You better clean dat pit. You does go and leggo fat fat leer in it! Clean it man! Lemme tell you someting, I wouda clean dat pit if a dog de shit in it. I wouda clean it because I know dat a dog not have sense. If a fowl or a cow de shit in de latrine, I wouda clean it. If a little chile de shit in it, I wouda take me hand and clean de chile shit. But is big people who shit in it. As God above, me Choonilal not cleanin dat pit. You have to clean dat latrine, Tailor!'

Then he gave a whole lecture on the uses and abuses of an outhouse. Folding his arms, he waited sadly on Tailor's reply.

The village queer couldn't stay out of it any more; it was his business to be up to date in village happenings. Since his wife, Rookmin, was not at home, Sook decided to close the shop and move over by Choonilal. He was old as Choonilal, but he was more fortunate; he had all his hair on his head. So Sook closed the shop and walked out on the road. He said to Choonilal, 'Like you havin trobble boy Choon?'

'Yeh man Sook, I havin trobble wid Tailor man.'

Then the queer turned to Tailor and asked, 'Like you havin trobble boy Tail?'

'Yeh man Sook, Choonilal playin in he modderass. De man want me to pay rent. He want me to clean dat latrine.

Sook was an expert when it came to village quarrels. He decided to side with Tailor and Choonilal at the same time. So he said, 'All you livin in one village man. All you must try and live good.'

But Choonilal felt that Sook was playing a dangerous game, talking to him and talking to Tailor at the same time. Choonilal said, 'Sook, tell Tailor to clean dat latrine.'

'I cant tell Tailor dat man Choon. I dont see why you makin all dat fuss about latrine and dis kinda kiss-me-ass ting, man Choon. Be a man, man. Just tell Poonwa dat you is a poor man. Tell him dat you dont have any money. Be a man, Choon.'

And Choonilal: 'Look Sook, keep you ass shut! Who talkin about Poonwa here? Dis quarrel have notten to do wid Poonwa or Poonwa passage to Canada. Oright!'

And Sook: 'You know dat is de Canada business dat worryin you, Choon. You know dat. Talk de truth as God above.'

Before Choonilal could speak, his wife Basdai dropped out of a taxi. She had gone to Tolaville to buy groceries; the Choonilals bought almost all their goods in Tolaville because Sook's prices were too high for them. Basdai was not surprised to see Choonilal and Tailor in war. She knew that Choonilal was going to do anything to prevent their son Poonwa from going to Canada. It was easy to see that there was a war on, because Tailor was standing under the chataigne tree with a worried face, and Choonilal was jumping all over the yard and talking to Sook. Basdai didn't like the idea of the queer talking to her husband; this was because Sook was one of the men who was telling Choonilal to call off the mortgage deal with Pandit Puru; in her opinion, this man was dangerous. She had a slight suspicion that Sook was trying to prevent Poonwa from going to Canada, because the queer wanted to drag her son into sodomy.

Basdai was afraid of Poonwa remaining in Karan Settlement. She had seen too many men fall victim to the evil designs of the village queer. Basdai believed in the Hindu Mission to Canada; she was positive that Poonwa was going to do well. She just couldn't see why Choonilal was against the idea; she couldn't see too what business the village queer had by interfering; not interfering alone, but taking it upon himself to advise Choonilal, advise him at great lengths just to prove that the Hindu Mission to Canada was going to be of no use. And not only Sook but Ragbir too, these men were worrying about Poonwa's mission more than Poonwa himself. So, from the time Basdai walked into the yard, she said to Sook, 'Wot de ass you doin here?'

'I come because Choon and Tail quarrellin!'

'You come here to make trobble! But wedder you try to put sense in Choonilal head or not, Poonwa goin to Canada. You hear dat. I is Poonwa modder and I say he goin to Canada! I want to see who de modderass go stop him from goin!'

And Sook: 'Ay woman, watch you mout! I just leff me shop and come here. I didn't tell you husban one kiss-me-ass ting. You hear dat!'

'Why you dont go and take man?' Basdai asked.

'I does take man wid me own ass, woman!' the queer shouted.

Choonilal didn't want Basdai to quarrel with Sook, because the queer was his friend. He would have mortgaged his property two months ago if it hadn't been for Sook. From the first day that Poonwa had talked to Choonilal about his mission to Canada, Sook had told Choonilal to watch it. Sook was an experienced man; he had been a businessman in Karan Settlement for thirty years. It was the queer who had told Choonilal that the village priest was only trying to get at his property. So Choonilal said to his wife, 'Look woman, you leff Sook alone. You hear. Sook not tellin me notten you know.'

Basdai wanted to know what had really happened. She said to Choonilal, 'Tell me wot worryin you ass, Choon?'

Choonilal thought a little, then he began to cry. He knew that Basdai was always a weak woman; she didn't have the constitution to stand weeping. Choonilal was certain that he would succeed, because thirty years ago when he had wanted to marry Basdai, she rejected him. He had tried and tried to get her to change her mind, but she was determined. But one day he started weeping and she became worried.

He had wept for days, until Basdai, fearing he would die of sorrow, married him. As he was crying and getting on, Basdai asked, 'O God Choon, wot you cryin for?'

'I cryin because Tailor cussin me since you gone Tolaville. He cussin and callin me dog. If you know how Tailor insultin me, Bass. O God, in me old days man cussin me and callin me dog ... '

Basdai said to Tailor, 'You modderass you! You cussin Choon! You eat he kiss-me-ass food and now you cussin him. You callin him dog. Look Tailor, haul you tail out a me house. Haul it!'

And Tailor: 'Basdai, I didnt cuss Choonilal. Since you leff de house, Choonilal gettin on wid me. Ask Sook. Is Choonilal who cussin me since day clean out. Ask Sook.'

And Sook: 'If all you want to get on and make trobble, den get on and make trobble. But dont call me name.

And Choonilal: 'Tailor, you cuss me. Talk de truth man, we is big people man Tailor man.'

Tailor admitted that he did curse Choonilal. But he said that he did it only when Choonilal kept on worrying him about the outhouse.

When Basdai heard about the outhouse she got mad. She had really never forgiven Tailor; she couldn't forgive him, because Tailor was responsible for the condition of the latrine; he was responsible for her having to take all that trouble to empty her bowels in the sugarcane field. So she said, 'Tailor!'

'Oy,' Tailor answered.

'Clean dat modderass latrine!'

'Who de modderass you bawlin at? Look Basdai, mind you kiss-me-ass mout. You know dat you and Choonilal used to shit in de damn blasted latrine. I willin to clean it, but Choonilal have to help me.'

'Choon dont have to help you at all! Choon didnt bring Phyllis dat whore to shit in it. You hear dat. Dat Phyllis done make enuff trobble in Tola aready. She come from a whole line of jamets. You dont know dat, Tailor. You not from Tola. She and she modder Leeza and she gran-modder Ama was de wost whores dat pass through Tola. De wost! Tola coud never have a family of jamets like dem. You dont know notten, Tailor! Dat same Phyllis dat takin man all over dis island was de same woman who cause a man to hang.'

Tailor didn't say anything, so Basdai took up the handbag of groceries and went inside the house. But something was still worrying her. She leaned over a window and said to Tailor, 'Clean dat latrine else I go put you outta me place.'

And Tailor: 'Under British Law you cant put me out!'

'British Law coud kiss me ass!'

'Let a policeman hear you say dat!'

'De policeman and British Law coud kiss me ass!'

Basdai slammed the window and pulled back her head inside the house. When Tailor mentioned British Law she became nervous. She had already felt the powers of the Law. Some twenty years ago she used to keep a brown cow in the yard. One morning when Choonilal got up to milk the cow, he started to bawl. The cow was missing. A villager told them that Ragbir stole the cow and gave it to some of his relatives in Curry Tola. Basdai decided to put Ragbir in the hands of the Law. She went to Tolaville and reported the case of the missing cow to the police. The Tolaville police, always slow when it came to urgent matters, acted as if there was no case at all. The police took about one month to reach to Curry Tola, although Curry Tola was only ten miles away. When the law had enquired about the cow, Ragbir's relative had already sold the cow to some butcher in Spanish City. So the police told Basdai that there was nothing she could do. But Basdai wanted to see Ragbir in jail, so she started a long court proceeding against him. The prospect of seeing her neighbour behind bars thrilled her. After all, it was Ragbir who had begun the scandal when Poonwa was born. In those days Ragbir used to make fun of the Choonilals. He told the people that Poonwa was not Choonilal's child, and Basdai was helpless. But when the cow incident came up, she decided to push the case. But the case was like any other case; it dragged on and on like any other too.

Suddenly it ended: Ragbir got away, and Basdai was fined one hundred dollars. So when Tailor talked about the powers of the Law, Basdai was glad to close the window.

After Basdai slammed the window, Tailor stood under the chataigne tree and brooded. The past with all its troubles and joy filtered through his mind. Until today he had lived a great life with the Choonilals. Sure they had quarrels in the past, like the time when Choonilal had made a joke and Tailor pushed him. Tailor just pushed him easy, but Choonilal was a weak man; he fell on the ground. Basdai had laughed at first, but when Choonilal began to weep she ran up to Tailor. She scraped Tailor with her nails. He got mad and threatened to bite out her nose. She being a coward woman started calling for help. Then the same evening there was joy again in the household; it was if nothing had happened.

But this morning Choonilal had come into his little room and told him that he needed rent. At first Tailor thought he was making a joke, because Choonilal had been in the habit of coming into his room and making jokes. But it was no joke; Choonilal was serious. Tailor got mad and told his landlord that he wasn't going to pay any rent. The rent revelation worried Tailor. Unable to spin further reflections, Tailor said, 'Under British Law, Choonilal, I go lost you ass in jail. Under British Law you have to pay me for livin under you house. I goin to sue you for every cent you have in you bald head ass!'

'You modderass you!' Choonilal shouted. 'You live by me and now you talkin about Law. Say praise God I give you food to eat. You nima-karam modderass!'

Sook took up for Tailor. The queer said, 'All you be careful. Maybe Tailor could really put all you in jail, yeh.'

This talk about the Law was really eating Basdai. She flung open the window again, and said, 'Ay Sook! Watch you ass you know. Wot de ass you talkin about jail? Answer me nuh?'

'Like you want man, Basdai!' the queer shouted.

'Yeh I want man Sook!' she shouted. 'God make me wid a hole to take man. But you is a man and you takin man. You shouda shame. Why you dont go and kill youself?'

This had a burning effect on the queer. It was all right if a man told him about his bad habits, but he couldn't take it from a woman. So he said, 'Man sweeter dan woman!'

This had a stinging effect on Basdai. A long time ago, the time when she couldn't have a child, Choonilal had become frustrated. Then the queer had told Choonilal that women were no good. Choonilal believed him. So Choonilal abandoned his wife and went into the full-time practice of sodomy. He and Sook used to have an affair every night. One night Ragbir came into the shop to buy something, and he saw Choonilal and Sook having an affair on the wooden counter. Ragbir with his unlimited capacity for mischief went and called some villagers. The people burst into the rum shop; they found Choonilal pumping Sook. The village priest asked Choonilal why he was having an affair with Sook when he had a young wife at home. At first Choonilal was so embarrassed that he couldn't talk. But Pandit Puru kept pounding him for the answer. Choonilal thought a little; he looked at his wife and at the queer, and said that Sook was sweeter than his wife. Basdai was so shocked that she fainted inside the shop. Now that Sook talked about the sweetness of men, Basdai couldn't argue with him; she just pulled back her head into the house.

Sook felt good. He was a man of unsound morals, but he had some goodness in his heart. He was in the habit of scanning the village with an eagle's eyes. Whenever a young man was in trouble, he was the first to lend a helping hand. And over a period of more than thirty years of work, the queer had developed his own peculiar way of settling quarrels with women; he knew exactly what to say to keep them quiet. The women couldn't argue with Sook; he was a professional when he came into an argument. Over the years he had accumulated a vast amount of experience with men; he had enjoyed more men than any woman in Karan Settlement could ever boast of. When Tailor came to Karan Settlement, the queer had supported Choonilal's idea of giving Tailor the little room. Before a week had time to pass, Sook and Tailor had been involved in more than ten affairs.

Sook was not an ungrateful man either; he was in the habit of helping out his lovers. After Phyllis had knocked down the eastern wall of the outhouse and Choonilal had threatened Tailor, threatened him and told him not to use the outhouse, Sook had invited Tailor to use his latrine. Sook didn't charge Tailor a rent for using the outhouse. But

Sook was a businessman; he had his own way of settling accounts. Every day when Tailor came to use the outhouse, Sook used to slip through the backdoor with a stout in his hand. As soon as Tailor came out of the latrine, Sook handed him the stout, played with him a little, and as Tailor's desire rose, they just slipped into the shop, and, bolting the door, enjoyed each other. Now that Basdai couldn't face him, Sook decided to make some noise. But he couldn't make noise. A taxi stopped. His wife Rookmin dropped out. From the time Sook saw her, he started to run. Rookmin was a serious woman. As Sook was running, she shouted, 'Dont run, you modderass! I done see you.'

Ragbir, Choonilal's eastern neighbour, sat on his bed and fanned himself with his favourite blue towel. He was a fat man in his early forties, and he had an appetite for confusion. All morning he had been sitting by his window with his bearded face hanging out of the house. He had followed minutely the development of the war that was ravaging the household of his western neighbours. He knew exactly why Choonilal had attacked Tailor; it was the Hindu Mission to Canada idea. Ragbir was pleased with the way things were going. All his life he had enjoyed the misfortune of others. When there was no confusion in the village, he used to scare the little children. He had a way of turning up his eyes; turning them in such a way as to make his eyeballs two red blobs. All morning he had been content to sit by the window and enjoy himself. Now he pulled his head in and closed the window. He took some Bay Rum and sapped his wiry beard. Then he took his favourite towel and wiped his face. While he was still on the bed, he contemplated the idea of death. He clutched his enormous testicles as he thought about the gloomy subject.

He was a worried man; all morning he had waited by the window for Choonilal; he wanted to talk to Choonilal about a dream he had had last night. Last night he had gone to bed early. Without saying his prayers, he fell asleep. In the night he dreamt that he was dead and the Aryan gods turned him into a snake. When he woke up, he decided to pray to them right away. But before he had time to finish his prayers, he fell asleep again and dreamt the monkey god Hanuman. Hanuman came to impart to him some kind of profound and secretive knowledge of the afterlife. But the visitation brought pain. The monkey god held on to Ragbir and squeezed his testicles. He woke from the dream and found his large hands squeezing his load of balls. Ragbir had waited and waited on Choonilal, but he never came. But he didn't mind, after all; he was able to enjoy the quarrel between Tailor and Choonilal. Now that Rookmin was getting on with Sook, he decided to leave the confinement of his little room and go over the road. Wrapping his blue towel around his head, he waddled out of his house.

Now Tailor was under attack by Rookmin and Choonilal. Rookmin said to Tailor, 'How much time you bull Sook? Which part you bull him, dat he come to talk to you so soon?'

And Tailor: 'Look, woman, watch you mout! I never bull Sook, you hear. You tink I is Choonilal to bull man, nuh. Oho.'

And Choonilal: 'I used to bull Sook long time, you hear dat, Tailor. Is years now I never bull Sook. I is a man of God, Tailor. You does bull Sook, because you does go and shit in he latrine every mornin.'

'I does shit in he latrine, but I dont bull him.'

Rookmin quarrelled a little more; she quarrelled and told Tailor not to use the latrine any more; she threatened that if ever she saw him by her outhouse, she would root out his testicles. She said how she was a full-grown woman; Tailor couldn't fool her. Then she left the yard and went into Choonilal's house to talk with Basdai; she left because Ragbir was already crossing over the new road to come and join in the battle of words. When Ragbir reached by the chataigne tree, he said, 'Boy Choon, dis life eh play, it have trobble nuh.'

'Yeh boy Rag, dis life have trobble too bad. Tailor man, de man shit in me latrine, man. God have mercy. Tailor shit fat fat leer in de pit man, boy Rag. Man Rag, I does feel to kill meself wen I smell dat pit in de night. Dis world have too much trobble man Rag man. I tellin you boy Rag. Sometimes in de night wen I get up to pray to God man Rag, I does cant pray man. Look, eh Rag, Tailor givin me too much trobble man.'

Ragbir scratched his balls and said, 'Boy Choon, dis life have plenty trobble, man. But Tailor shouda have enuff sense to know dat he livin by you man Choon. It not good to take advantage, man.'

And Tailor: 'I willin to clean dat latrine, but Choonilal have to help me.'

'You modderass! I go help you?'

'Yeh Choonilal, you have to help me!'

'O God, Ragbir, hear how dat dog talkin to me ... '

Choonilal couldn't continue; he was weeping.

When Tailor saw Choonilal in tears, he began to laugh. It was nothing very surprising about the weeping Choonilal; tears had always been a secret weapon for Choonilal. Then Tailor began to sing an Indian song as he walked to his little room.

Choonilal and Ragbir left the yard and came under the house. They sat on the little bench and talked. First Ragbir told Choonilal about the strange dream he had last night, told him how Hanuman came and squeezed his testicles and caused him to scream. Choonilal listened, then he interpreted the dream, saying, 'You is a blessed man, Rag. To get a good dream like dat it mean Hanuman like you, because you done do enuff good in de world. Wen you dead, it mean dat you goin to live wide de gods in heaven, Rag.'

Ragbir complained, 'But I bawl out wen de god squeeze me stones, Choon.'

'Don't bawl out next time, Rag. It is a blessin if a god squeeze you stones while you sleepin.'

But deep down inside, Choonilal was uneasy. For about two months now he had been praying for Ragbir every day, just because he was using Ragbir's outhouse; he knew that the monkey god had visited Ragbir because of his prayers. Choonilal cursed himself secretly for the prayers he had offered to the gods for his fat neighbour. Not wishing Ragbir to detect his thoughts, Choonilal began to weep again.

Rookmin was a fat, reddish woman in her forties. She had married Sook some thirty years ago. Before she married, she had no idea that Sook was a queer. It was a few days after her marriage that she found out. At first she toyed with the idea of leaving Sook, but she couldn't.

Sook was a good man in many ways: he never drank rum like some of the villagers, and he never beat her up. In those days, Choonilal used to drink and beat up Basdai all over Karan Settlement, but Sook never touched Rookmin. But the most important reason why she never left him was because of his ability to do business. Sook was a born shop-keeper. He had a way of dealing with accounts; for example, if a villager owed him ten dollars, Sook never quarrelled with the villager for his money. He allowed some time to pass. Then one day he would ask the villager to pay something on the account. If the villager hesitated, Sook would give him a stout or a drink of rum free. When the villager under-stood that the shopkeeper was his friend, then Sook would come back again to the embarrassing question of accounts. With a good heart Sook would tell the villager that he owed him fifty dollars. The villager would take out his eyes and say that he only owed him about twenty dollars. Sook would offer him another stout and tell him that it was fifty dollars. Then Sook would talk about God and death and so on, and the villager would pay him. This was the important reason why Rookmin had stayed with Sook all these years.

Today Rookmin was eager to interfere in the personal business of the Choonilals. For about thirty years they had lived as neighbours; they had always been close. Poonwa's Hindu Mission to Canada pleased her a lot. Rookmin had seen too many young men with talent waste away. All the young scholars in Karan Settlement were doomed. The sugarcane estates were monsters; they were in the habit of yawning and swallowing the young men; those who were lucky enough to get away from the estates were trapped into a career of rum drinking and fighting. Rookmin felt that Poonwa had some talent; she sided with Basdai to send him to Canada. Rookmin didn't want Basdai's son to come out like Tailor. Rookmin had never particularly liked Tailor. He was really a man of mystery. He had just shown up in Karan Settlement with a black notebook in which was written hundreds of names, names of people in various villages. Whenever a person questioned Tailor's family descent, he was always able to furnish yards and yards of genea-logical connections: he had an aunt here and an uncle there, and so on. For two whole months she had seen Tailor using her outhouse. She knew that he was having an affair with Sook; she didn't mind the affair too much, but she had a feeling that her husband was giving away things from the shop. She climbed up the steps and called, 'Ay Bass, where you is?'

'I cleanin out de front room gal Rook. Come nuh.'

Rookmin went inside the room and sat on the bed. The bed was very untidy. Rookmin said, 'Huh, like you and Choon de doin it last night gal. How de bed like dis?'

'Nuh gal,' Basdai said. 'Last night whole night Choon couldnt sleep. We too old now to do rudeness. We leff dat for yong people.'

'It good to do it sometime, gal,' Rookmin said.

Basdai laughed and declared, 'You know how long we never do it? Lemme see. Look I cant remember, gal. Yeh I remember now. Since Poonwa talk about he mission, we never do it.'

'Well dat is a long time,' Rookmin said.

The Hindu Mission to Canada was really causing all the trouble in the house.

'I dont know why Choon worryin so much,' Basdai said. 'I tink it is a good ting for Poonwa to go over.'

'It is a blasted good ting, yeh,' Rookmin said. 'I dont see why Chooni-lal makin all dat trobble for, man. If Poonwa coud go over and teach white people about Hinduism, it is a good ting. Gal Bass, if I was in you position, I wouda give Choon pressure in he ass. He shouda glad to know dat he chile want to do someting good in de world.'

And Basdai: 'Pressure is joke. Choon dont know de woman he playin wid. Gal Rook, I go stand up on Choon windpipe till he get dat money. One kiss-me-ass chile I have in dis world. Man I is Poonwa modder, and I done tell Choon dat Poonwa have to go to Canada. I goin to give Choon pressure so, till he shit in he pants. You tink I want Poonwa to live in Karan Settlement? Yong people have no future in Karan Settlement. Look how all dem yong yong boys drinkin rum in de village. I tell you, gal Rook, Choon have to pull out dat money and give it to Poon.'

'Man I tell you, Bass,' Rookmin said, 'I tell you dese men and dem playin in dey ass.'

'You see, gal Rook, is Sook and Ragbir who tellin Choon not to send Poon to Canada. But wedder dey jump high or low, gal Rook, Poon goin to Canada.'

'You right yeh, gal Bass. Poonwa is you chile. Try and get him outta dis village yeh. Odderwise, he go end up drinkin rum. Look I tell you, ever day gal Bass, all dem yong boys from Tola does come in de rum shop. Some of dem went to college and ting, gal. Dey comin in de shop and drinkin rum like worta. Look gal, I does surprise to see. Even dem schoolteachers drinkin rum all over de place, gal.'

Basdai said that college boys and schoolteachers were the greatest rum drinkers in Carib Island. She pointed out that labourers on the sugar estates couldn't cope with the teachers. According to her, there were some teachers who spent all their salary on rum.

Rookmin was willing to add something to the list of rum drinkers. She said that lawyers were beginning to surpass schoolteachers as rum drinkers. She said that the lawyers in some of the country districts were in the habit of fighting cases for a few bottles of rum. A ready example, one that Basdai knew about also, came to Rookmin's mind. She told Basdai about the lawyer who lived in Chaggyville. He had a white wife. In the night he and his wife used to undress and run through the back streets naked. Every night the young men in Chaggyville used to drag the white woman inside the sugarcane field and seduce her. The lawyer was a very brilliant man. He was educated at Oxford in England, but rum made him stupid.

'Man Rook,' Basdai continued, 'I dont want Poonwa to stay in dis place. De only future in dis island is drinkin rum and playin de ass. By de hook or de crook, Poonwa goin on dat mission, gal.'

With a slow determination, Basdai drifted deeper and deeper into her private affairs. And she spoke with great hope too. She was certain that in a short time she was going to apply enough pressure to her husband to make him agree to the Hindu Mission to Canada.

Remembering that Poonwa was working as a clerk in Spanish City, Rookmin asked, 'Poonwa workin five years now. How come he dont have money?'

Instead of resting the blame on the extravagant shoulders of her son, Basdai allowed it to rest on the shoulders of Poonwa's employer. She reminded Rookmin that Poonwa was only a clerk, a lawyer's clerk too besides. She complained how the Madrassi lawyer was a stingy man. He used to pay Poonwa only ten dollars a week. Poonwa spent more than five dollars a week in travelling from Karan Settlement to Spanish City. Then Poonwa had to buy his lunch in Spanish City. It was not hard for Rookmin to believe this. She knew that lawyers paid their clerks small salaries.

'Well, in dat case, he cant have no money. I tell you gal Bass, dese lawyers in dis island is some modderass yeh. Dey does just play dey know Law and ting, but I tell you. Look at dat Madinga bitch in Tolaville. You know how much poor poor Indian and creole people he tief to get rich so. And who help him tief? Is lawyers help him tief. Or look at dat case in Benwa Settlement. Balky take de rope behind dat Lawyer Gobin. In de end, Phyllis lost she house and everyting. Dese lawyers is really some modderass!'

Then Basdai sat on the bed next to Rookmin and told her why Choonilal was getting on. She said that Choonilal was scared – scared of losing his property to the priest.

'You tink dat Pandit Puru go tief de house and land gal?' Rookmin asked.

'I dont know gal Rook,' Basdai said.

'Me eh tink dat Pandit go do dat.'

'Me eh tink so eidder. But you know how Choon does worry about everyting, gal. He feel dat Pandit only offerin dat money because he want to tief out wot we have.'

Rookmin stayed a little longer and listened to Basdai. Then she encouraged her to give Choonilal trouble until he agreed to the Mission idea. When she was convinced that Basdai would continue to battle Choonilal, she said, 'I goin home now. I goin and see wot to cook gal.'

'Oright,' Basdai said.

As Rookmin walked down the steps, she saw Ragbir and Choonilal sitting on the wooden bench and talking. When Ragbir saw her, he got up from the bench and came by the step. Pushing his fat head out, he tried to see under her dress. Rookmin laughed and said, 'Behave you fat ass nuh Rag. If you like to see wot woman have so much, why you dont get a wife?'

Ragbir scratched his beard and said, 'God gal Rook, you does drive me mad gal.'

Choonilal was sitting on the bench and sweating, sweating as if he had been working all day. Rookmin knew that Ragbir was trying to convince Choonilal that the Hindu Mission to Canada was not a good thing. She looked at Choonilal and said, 'Dont worry boy Choon, Poon go do oright in Canada man. You chile have brains man Choon. Try and help him.'

Choonilal didn't say anything, so Rookmin left.

Poonwa came from work at 3 p.m. He crossed over the main road and walked into the yard. Choonilal and Ragbir were still sitting on the bench and talking. Poonwa looked at his father and asked, 'Did you get the money, Father?'

Choonilal was silent. Ragbir decided to speak. He said, 'Boy Poon, you fadder worried, man.'

Poonwa knew that Ragbir was seriously against the Hindu Mission to Canada. He hated Ragbir. Poonwa shouted, 'Get your fat-ass arse out of here! It is none of your business to interfere. Get out now!'

'Man Poon, behave youself nuh,' Ragbir said

This got Poonwa mad. He walked up to Ragbir and pointing a folded fist at his face, he said, 'Now you go right out. Come on!'

Ragbir knew that Poonwa was serious. He got up and left.

'Father!'

'Wot you want, Poon?' Choonilal asked.

'Did you get the money?'

'No. But … '

'No excuses! What do you think a mission is? Well, let me tell you something, Father, a mission is a great thing. For too long the whiteman came with his principles and bullshit. Canada sent out a mission for

Hindus. What did that mission do, Father? Well, I'll tell you what it did. It taught Indians how to worship the values of the white world. It taught them that their philosophy and their whole way of life was wrong. The mission didn't educate them in their own language. It taught them to read and write in English. This is the reason why these coming generations are lost. And the Negro is in no better position. First the whiteman made him a slave. He beat him and tortured him until everything about Africa was killed. Then he abolished him. Today both Indian and Negro exist without culture. They are a lost people. They are mimics.'

Choonilal had worked all his life on Indian Estate. For him the whiteman was a god. He said to Poonwa, 'Dont talk about white people so.'

Poonwa thought a little. Then he said, 'Cogito ergo sum!'

The beauty of the sentence swept Choonilal off his feet. He laughed and said, 'Boy Poon, you really bright. You could talk English like a Englishman.

'That is Latin, Father!'

'I de tink it was English boy Poon.'

Choonilal was an illiterate man, but good English had always made him happy. Once when Poonwa came first in a public speaking contest in Spanish City, Choonilal had been so overwhelmed that he wept for a day and a night. Basdai, being a nervous woman, thought that Choonilal was going to weep to death. Gathering her courage in one heap, she went to Tolaville and got a young Indian doctor to look after Choonilal. The East Indian doctor was new to the practice; he was on the lookout for special cases. Armed with a black bag in which there was cotton and needles, the young doctor came to Karan Settlement. The doctor told Basdai to remain in the hall. He went inside Choonilal's room and closed the door. At first Basdai heard the doctor and her husband talking in the room. Then a deadly silence had stepped in. Fearing that the doctor had had the courage to allow Choonilal to die, Basdai burst into the room. But there was no need for alarm. Choonilal had told the doctor about the public speaking contest. The man of medicine had been so impressed with the report on Poonwa's eloquence that he had forgotten himself. He was content to sit on the bed next to Choonilal and weep with his patient.

'Look, Father, we don't have time for cock-and-bull stories. When are you going to have the money?'

Choonilal wanted to get away from the money issue. He knew that Poonwa always came from work around 6 p.m. But today he was at home at 3 p.m. This bothered Choonilal, so he asked, 'How you come home so soon, Poonwa?'

Poonwa said that he didn't have the guts to work any more. He said how the Madrassi lawyer was in the habit of exploiting him, working him long hours and paying him only ten dollars a week.

'Well, look for anodder job,' Choonilal advised.

'I'm not going to look for another job, Father. I need the money to go on my Mission. I am already twenty-five years old. It is time I leave this island, Father.'

'But which part I go get de money boy Poon?'

This drove Poonwa mad. He screamed, 'Do you want me to stay on this island and drink rum, Father? You know that the educated men on this island are drifting more and more into a career of rum drinking. Soon we will become a nation of rum drinkers!'

Suddenly it dawned upon Choonilal that he was a disgrace to his son. Poonwa was a philosopher and a master of many languages; his father was an unlettered peasant. The ghost of his own neglect came back to haunt him. Before Poonwa was born, Choonilal had been a man of some ambition. As he stood in front of Poonwa, he thought about the time he had wanted to learn English; that had been a few weeks after he had gone bald suddenly. When Choonilal went bald he had realized for the first time in his life that it was not good for a man to toil under the sun. After this accident of nature, he had developed a hate for cane-cutting. One day he was cutting cane on Indian Estate; he was cutting the cane bare-headed and bald-headed; sweat was falling from his forehead; his shirt was wet; and the driver was yelling at him. Without even telling his wife about his plans, he dropped the cutlass and ran out of the estate. Basdai thought that he had gone to empty his bowels somewhere in the sugarcane field. But Choonilal hadn't gone to empty his bowels; he just ran out of that sugar plantation and went in the rum shop and sat down. Sook had asked him what was wrong;

with his hands on his hips, the queer stood and waited for him to speak. At first Choonilal didn't know what to say; he really had no proper reason for leaving the work on the estate. Then Choonilal had an idea. He told Sook that he wanted to learn to read and write in English. It had interested the queer to learn that his neighbour had been willing to spend a few hours with him. Sook wrote the alphabet on a sheet of brown paper and tried his best with his pupil. Then Sook gave Choonilal some rum to drink. When Choonilal got a little tipsy, Sook had closed the shop, and they went to the Anglican Church. It was Choonilal's first affair of the kind. Perhaps he would have learnt English; Sook had been a good instructor. But in those days Choonilal had been more interested in Sodomy.

Then Choonilal thought of that morning two months ago when Poonwa woke up and began screaming for his father and mother. Basdai and Choonilal thought that Tailor was murdering Poonwa, because the latrine incident was only a day old. So Choonilal took a cutlass and he and his wife ran into Poonwa's room. Poonwa's face was red and swollen; it was as if something terrible had happened to him. Poonwa was breaking wind hard hard and getting on. It took the Choonilals a long time to understand what their son was saying. Finally it dawned upon them that Poonwa needed five thousand dollars to go to Canada. He told them that the white world needed the Mission. Basdai liked the idea; she had always hoped that Poonwa would make up his mind to leave Karan Settlement. But Choonilal was mad. He complained that he had no money. Then Poonwa told him to mortgage the house and get the money. Choonilal was mad to hear that; he had worked all his life just to build the house and buy the land.

Overburdened by memories, Choonilal wept.

'Why are you weeping, Father?'

'I cryin because I dont have de money to give you, Poon. You know dat I dont have money, but you want money.'

'Get the money, I say!' Poonwa yelled.

Choonilal felt a sudden pain in his belly. The desire to defecate was so strong that he started to run.

'Where are you going, Father?'

'I goin to shit by Ragbir!'

Poonwa went and knocked at Tailor's door. 'Leff me alone nuh Chooni-lal!' Tailor said.

'It is Poonwa,' Poonwa said.

Tailor opened the door for Poonwa. Poonwa went and sat on Tailor's canvas cot. Tailor sat on a chair by the sewing machine. Then Tailor asked, 'Choon give you de money?'

'No. Father is a real dummy. I cannot get a straight answer from the man. He can get the money if he really wants to.'

'Choonilal playin in he ass, man Poon. De man coud more dan give you de money to go over, man. Lemme tell you someting. Since mornin you fadder quarrellin about dat latrine. You know why he quarrellin? He dont want to give you dat money. De old people and dem have a sayin: wen goat shit want to roll, it does wait for a breeze. Dat is de same ting Choonilal doin. But give him pressure in he ass, Poon. Hand him pressure man.'

Tailor was in favour of Poonwa's Hindu Mission to Canada. He knew that Basdai and Choonilal loved Poonwa; he was their only child. Tailor knew that if Poonwa really left the island, he would have a good chance to live comfortably with the Choonilals.

'I will do all in my power to get that money,' Poonwa said.

Poonwa left Tailor's room and went upstairs to talk to his mother. Basdai was cooking in the kitchen. As soon as she saw her son, she said, 'How you come home so early, Poon?'

'I have left the job, Mother.'

'So how early you want to go over?'

'I have to leave this island soon, Mother.'

Basdai said, 'Well, dat is just now. You fadder still don't want to give dat money. He still sayin dat he not goin to mortgage de property.'

'Well, Mother, he'd better change his mind.'

Basdai wanted to see Poonwa out of Karan Settlement. A long time ago, she had made all the plans for Poonwa. Choonilal never wanted Poonwa to attend school; he wanted him to work on the sugarcane estate. It was Basdai who had the courage in those days to speak up for Poonwa. She had to wage a constant battle against Choonilal. When Poonwa completed his elementary education, Choonilal wanted him to learn a trade: mechanic or welding or something like that. Again Basdai had to use her influence and prove to her husband that it was better for Poonwa to go to college. She had carried the matter too far to fall down now. She said to Poonwa, 'I have a plan, Poon.'

Ragbir was sitting on his bed and fanning himself with the blue towel. He knew that Choonilal was going to run away from Poonwa. With a great amount of satisfaction, he watched Choonilal, watched him as he bolted across the road. As Choonilal passed under his window, Ragbir said, 'Wot happen boy Choon?'

But Choonilal couldn't answer. The pain in his belly was really strong. He just gave Ragbir a little glance and ran to the outhouse. Choonilal pulled down his pants and sat on the wooden seat. He didn't bother to close the door; he had never closed the door since he had been using Ragbir's pit. It was a habit of Choonilal's to leave the door open. It was Ragbir's habit, too, to lean over his window and look at Choonilal. While Choonilal was defecating, Ragbir leaned out and asked, 'How you shittin so boy Choon?'

'Man Rag, wot I go tell you, man. Me son so educated dat wen he talk, I does only feel to shit, man. Dey boy talk some Latin just now man Rag. Man wen I hear de Latin, a shit take me one time.'

'Befo you hit de boy a good slap in he ass, Choon. De modderass, you mind de chile from small and bring him big, now he talkin Latin. Man Choon, you happy yeh. If Poon was me chile, I wouda done kick him in he ass. Long time I wouda done wring out he stones. Man Choon, I tell you, dis island is someting else, man. Dese yong Indian boys and dem, dey drinkin rum and talkin English too bad, man. De more dey does drink rum is de more dey does talk English.'

Choonilal said, 'Just now you go see wot go happen in dis island, Rag. Everybody in dis island want to go to school. Nobody dont want to work in de cane or plant tomatoes and ting, you know boy. All of dem want big work in govament and ting. All of dem want to be police and postman and ting, boy Rag. Just now in dis island it go have so much educated people dat dey go have to take dey G.C.E. and ting and wipe dey ass, Rag. Just now, man, wid Cambridge Certificates have to eat shit. Dat time is just round de corner. Who live dey go see.'

Choonilal had finished defecating a few minutes ago, but he continued to sit on the wooden seat. Silently he was praying to the Aryan gods. Reluctantly, he asked them to bless Ragbir, because Ragbir was kind enough to allow him to use his pit. Then he moved on to the more important topic. He begged Hanuman to leave his place in the sky and come down to Karan Settlement. He asked the monkey god to do something to make Poonwa change his mind about the Hindu Mission to Canada. While he still talking to the gods, he heard Ragbir saying something. Choonilal ended the prayer and asked, 'Wot you say boy Rag?'

'Why you dont tell Bass to come and use me latrine too.'

This was a serious invitation. Choonilal knew that Ragbir was a lecherous man; he had committed many rapes in Karan Settlement. So Choonilal said, 'Me wife like to shit home, boy Rag.'

'Which part home?' Ragbir asked.

Choonilal remembered that his outhouse was out of order. But he said, 'She does shit upstairs in the de toilet, man.'

Ragbir, still fanning himself with his favourite blue towel, said, 'Dont try to fool me, Choon. Basdai does shit in de canefield man.'

It surprised Choon to hear that Ragbir knew so much about his wife.

'Sappose a man hold she down? Sappose a man leggo some totey on she one night, boy Choon?'

Remembering the night that the taxidriver had raped Basdai, Choonilal took out his eyes. He had never told Ragbir that Basdai was emptying her bowels in the canefield. Choonilal coughed a little, then he asked, 'How you know dat me wife does shit in de cane, man Rag?'

'I livin in Karan Settlement boy Choon. You tink I livin one hundred miles from here. You livin right over de road. If you wife does shit in de cane, I must know dat. I not dead yet you know, Choon.'

Then Ragbir, with his capacity for mischief, asked, 'Like you tinkin about de time you and Basdai de stick up like dogs, boy Choon?'

Choonilal had no problem remembering the incident. It had happened a long time ago – even before Poonwa was born. Basdai and Choonilal had wanted a child. After they were married, years had passed and Basdai wasn't getting pregnant. The idea of a childless marriage drove Choonilal to consult Pandit Puru. The priest had listened to Choonilal's story, then advised him accordingly. He told Choonilal that it was ungodly to have sex inside a house. The Aryan gods didn't like people who did their screwing indoors. Choonilal thought that Pandit Puru had given him the solution to his problem. He went by the riceland and built a little shed. Every evening when he and Basdai came from work, they used to go in the little shed and cohabit. But Basdai was a very nervous woman when it came around to outdoor sex. She was never comfortable with her husband in the shed; she constantly felt that someone would discover them in the act. Once while they were going at it with all their might, something ran in the bushes. Basdai got frightened. But Choonilal told her that it was nothing. When the affair was over, Choonilal had the surprise of his life: his organ had got trapped inside her. Choonilal pulled and pulled and tugged and tugged; he pulled and pulled and called on the Aryan gods, but it was of no use.

As the minutes ticked away, a great pain throbbed through Choonilal's organ. Choonilal rolled out of the shed with his wife. But still it was of no use. The idea of dying in such a position had crossed Choonilal's mind; he couldn't. So the Choonilals decided to face a village scandal. They bawled and called for help. Ragbir heard the screaming and went by the riceland. When Choonilal explained what had happened, Ragbir went to Karan Settlement to get some help. When the people heard of the dilemma the Choonilals were in, they came running to the riceland. With laughter and tears the villagers examined the situation. Laughing, Pandit Puru explained to the villagers that it was no laughing matter. Then the priest sent Ragbir to get soap and water. He massaged their organs. After a long massaging with soap and water Choonilal finally pulled out his totey. It was swollen like a horse's organ; it couldn't fit inside his pants. So Choonilal ran through the village with his exposed totey swinging from side to side.

'Man Rag, you dont play you have a good memory, nuh. Dat is wot you go talk about. Tell me wot to do wid Poonwa, nuh man.'

Wiping his face with the favourite blue towel, Ragbir said, 'Give Poonwa pressure in he ass, Choon. All you have in dis life is you house and you little piece of land. Dont allow you son to make you mortgage dat, man. Have you head on boy Choon.'

Choonilal said, 'Boy Rag, Poon really playin in he ass yeh. Wot de ass he want to go and teach white people about Hinduism? Tell me nuh, boy? White people bad nuh ass, yeh. Hitler was a whiteman, you know Rag. I tell you dem Jawmans kill people too bad in de war yeh. White people is real criminal you know boy Rag. Man, dey kill one anodder like rain, man.'

Ragbir didn't want to think about killing and death, so he scratched his balls and said, 'Hitler coud kiss me ass! Befo you studyin about Jawmans and dis kinda shit, you shoulda study wot to do wid Poonwa.'

'Tell me wot to do nuh boy Rag,' Choonilal said helplessly.

'Hit de boy a good lash in he ass man! He is a big man now, he coud take a lash in he ass. Now, you done shit boy Choon?'

'O God boy Rag, lemme siddown little bit nuh, man. Just now wen I dead, den nobody eh go have de cause to shit in you latrine. Den you go feel good.'

At last, mumbling something to the Aryan gods, Choonilal came out of the outhouse. As he walked to the road he said to his neighbour, 'Let we talk little bit nuh man Rag.'

'Look, Choonilal, haul you tail and go home. Go now befo I take a cutlass and chop up you ass yeh.'

Choonilal knew that he couldn't joke with Ragbir, because of what had happened once when Ragbir and Sook had had an affair. The queer had promised Ragbir twenty dollars. But after the affair was over, Sook had the boldness to say that he had no money. That drove Ragbir mad. With a cutlass in his hand, he chased the queer through the village. When Sook realized that Ragbir had been serious, he was glad enough to pay him the twenty dollars. Shaking his head, Choonilal muttered, 'Oright boy Rag. Lemme go and hear wot Poonwa have to say.'

Fingering his loose testicles, Ragbir leaned over the window and said, 'Boy Choon, I was just makin a joke, man.'

After Poonwa left his mother in the kitchen, he went inside his bedroom and stripped himself. He sat in the nude and thought about the past. Poonwa had become a pupil at Tolaville Canadian Mission School at the age of five. He had always thought that school would be a pleasant place. But when he entered school, he found out that there was nothing pleasant about it. At first he was very backward; it took him three years to learn the alphabet. There had been a white schoolmistress, a Canadian blond; it was her job to teach the infants. She was a heavy woman with a large bottom. She used to jump up and down like a mule and flog the children severely. Full of apostolic conviction, she used her teaching job as a platform to wage war against the heathen children.

She was precise; with her blue eyes she saw the Hindu children journeying to hell and the young Christians marching to heaven. She did all in her power to sustain the Christian march. She never flogged a Christian convert. But for the Hindus there was always the rod; they were going to hell anyway. Sometimes she used to offer sweets to the Hindu children. When they reached out to take one, she pulled back her hand and said, 'Sweets are only for those who love Jesus.' She knew a lot about hell and heaven and the devil and God. Many times she would stand up on a table and talk about Jesus. She knew a lot about the Bible too. For her, Jesus was the Lamb of God and the King of the Jews at the same time. He was a Jew in English fashion: blond hair, blue eyes, red beard, and a pink face.

Sometimes the power of the Lord used to come upon her. Bouncing around the room, she talked about miracles. Jesus made wine with water; He healed the sick with ease. Jesus was a baker too; He fed the multitude with the bread He had made. He made the bread just by clos-ing His eyes and mumbling something to His Father in heaven; when He opened them again, there it was. His Father in heaven felt that bread alone was no good, so fry fish was added to the menu. Poonwa was confused about Jesus. He had a mother called Mary. She was a virgin. Jesus had no father; He was a bastard. When Jesus was twelve years old, He was already a scholar; He had argued with doctors and lawyers, and had won His arguments too. He was a shepherd who took care of sheep. He had a great following, consisting of fishermen and prostitutes. As a young man He was a carpenter and an apprentice to His stepfather Joseph. All His life He was so busy that He never really found the time to make a bench or anything. He suffered from insomnia; He used to walk all night on the hills. He was a believer in peace; only once did He lose His temper. One day He took a whip and flogged the money lenders. The money lenders couldn't strike back, because the twelve fishermen were dangerous men; Peter used to carry a sword and Judas carried silver to take the Master's bail if the need should arise. Jesus even raised Lazarus from the dead, with the help of His Father who lived in heaven in those days.

Sometimes the Canadian blond would break out in long sessions of hymn singing. Her favourite was:

Jesus loves me
This I know
For the Bible tells me so.
Little ones to him belong;
They are weak, but He is strong.

When she sang, her blue eyes would glow and her big breasts would heave with emotion, but if a heathen child tried to sing along with her, she would get mad and hit his hands sharply with a ruler.

In those days Poonwa wanted to become a Christian; he was willing to do anything to get away from the beatings. Every day Poonwa used to get licks. Every evening when he came home he showed Choonilal and Basdai his swollen bottom. They told him that the blond was beating him because she loved him. One day when the blond really scared him, Poonwa came home and told his parents that he wanted to convert to Jesus. Choonilal had always been a religious Hindu; for him Christianity was something that was strange and weak: the Aryan gods were warriors, Jesus was a Lamb. He gave Poonwa a good beating and said there was no way he was going to allow him to forsake the Aryan gods. When Poonwa found out that he couldn't become a follower of the Man who changed water into wine, he looked for a way to escape the Canadian blond. Sometimes when the teacher was busy flogging the other heathens, he used to sneak through the back door of the school and hide in the outhouse. The school's outhouse was always filthy; there were scraps of brown paper and copybook pages with waste sticking to them scattered on the floor. There were flies too, millions of them; they maintained a steady buzz inside the wooden hut. Though the flies bothered him, Poonwa was happier with them than with the white schoolteacher. As the days passed, Poonwa became adjusted to the smell in the outhouse. The toilet was a safe place; there was no one to slap him and strike him with whips.

Lying down on the bed, Poonwa remembered how one day he had been sitting in the outhouse and had suffered an attack of hunger. Pulling out his roti from his pocket, he had begun to eat greedily inside the latrine. While he was chewing, a large blue fly dived inside his mouth. Poonwa spat out the food, then he started vomiting. One of his schoolmates heard the noise and told the teacher that there was someone vomiting inside the outhouse. The white woman thought that some Christian child was having difficulties with his bowels, so she ran out of the school to the rescue. She called out to Jesus as she pulled open the door and saw a heathen vomiting there in the darkness. She grabbed Poonwa and flung him in the bamboo grass. Poonwa was screaming and getting on as if he was sick. This drove the teacher mad with fury. She dragged Poonwa into the schoolroom. Then she went and whispered something to the headmaster, an East Indian who had been converted to serve the blue-eyed Jew. When he heard that a heathen had been eating in the toilet, his dark Madrassi face almost turned white, but he was too black for that. Then the headmaster and the schoolteacher carried Poonwa into the little room that was built as the flogging house of the heathens. Taking down Poonwa's pants and strapping him to a bench, the two Christians flogged him just as Christ had flogged the money lenders.

For months Poonwa couldn't sit properly. For months and months he tried to learn the alphabet, but the letters made no sense. In those days he cried and shouted that he didn't want to attend school. Choonilal was willing to take him out of school and send him to learn a trade, mechanics or welding, but Basdai used her influence. She had the feeling that Poonwa was going to get a fine education if he stayed at the Canadian Mission School.

At the end of three years, the headmaster got so fed up with Poonwa that he promoted him to first standard. Once Poonwa was out of the reach of the blond, he got along well in school and even blossomed into a brilliant pupil.

Poonwa got up from the bed. He went to his student desk and got his notebook and a pencil. He kept the notebook to record his thoughts and ideas about many subjects. Sitting on the bed again, he wrote in the notebook:

*The philosophy of Poonwa.*
*A treatise on God and other matters.*
*Philosophy and the philosopher's stones. (Women excluded.)*
*What goes in must come out. (Related to pregnancy and such matters.)*
*Philosophy and the philosophers' stones (Women excluded.)*
*The philosophy of a philosopher's hole (Women included.)*
*Once there was a girl*
*With two cracks in her hole*
*She pissed in a bowl.*
*Until she grew old.*

Poonwa lit a cigarette and smoked slowly. Then he took up his pencil and wrote in the journal:

*The Hindu Mission to Canada.*

He dragged deeply on his cigarette and added:

*I will go into the white country with the Hindu Bible and the whip. The white Christians came with their Bibles and whips and they succeeded just like that. I will take the Bhagavad Gita with me and open a school in Canada and employ East Indian teachers. I will build a torture chamber in the school.*

Then Poonwa began to brood over his school days. When he had completed his elementary education in the Mission School at Tolaville, he was offered a job as a monitor in the school. He had grabbed at it. But there was a condition to the job; he had to become a Christian. Poonwa went home and told his parents that he was going to get the job; they just had to give him consent to become a Christian. But Choonilal was going to have none of that. The Canadian schoolteacher peeped at Poonwa again. He saw her lifting her strong white arm to flog him, and he wrote quickly in his journal:

*Questions and Answers.*
*Ques… Are the angels male or female?*
*Ans…. I never peeped between an angel's legs.*
*Ques… Name one miracle.*
*Ans…. Mary was still a virgin after Jesus passed through her legs.*

Reading over what he had written, Poonwa nodded with satisfaction. Some day, after he was dead, his notebooks would be published, and all the world would know his private thoughts.

Tailor had given him the idea of keeping a journal. Lighting another cigarette, Poonwa began to worry about Tailor. When Tailor first came to Karan Settlement, Poonwa had already been working in Spanish City. One evening when he returned from work, he saw a strange man in the little room downstairs. Thinking that the man was a thief, Poonwa ran upstairs to tell Choonilal about it. But Choonilal told him that he had nothing to fear; the man downstairs was a poor tailor; destiny and poverty had brought him to Karan Settlement. Then Poonwa had gone downstairs with the hope of talking some philosophy with Tailor. But he had been disappointed. Tailor knew very little about books. Tailor had been a secretive man in those days. He was a small man too, the kind of people who have the stamina for meditation. Tailor knew a lot of Indian film songs. All night he had whistled and sung downstairs. Poonwa had hated Choonilal for being so stupid. But one day his hate vanished. While talking to Tailor one evening, Tailor showed him the black notebook in which he kept names and addresses of the various people who had patronized his laziness. He advised Poonwa to buy a notebook to record his thoughts. Poonwa had already filled up more than twenty-five notebooks with his thoughts and meditations.

Going back to bed, he caressed the scars that he had on his body. There was a particularly long one; he had got that from the Canadian blond that day she had taken him to the torture room. She didn't have a strap or a belt; she had a thin cable. She had strapped him to the bench and struck him with the cable. She was a strong woman. Poonwa had felt the cable, then he had fainted. When he woke up he had been shocked to discover a long bandage on his bottom. Then there had been pain for days. He had told his parents about the cut. Choonilal had said that it was good; the white woman was flogging him because she wanted him to be a good pupil.

To make matters worse, one day his father paid the school a visit. When Choonilal saw the white woman he was shocked; he had never spoken to a white woman before. He gave her instruction to flog Poonwa to her liking. As Poonwa thought about the incident, he pulled out the white woman from the cell of his mind. He strapped her mentally to the bench, then he took a fat cable and flogged her. Mentally he saw the long line of blood; he felt good. He placed the bleeding blond back into her cell. It gave Poonwa a certain amount of satisfaction to realize that he had kept her all these years in his mind. Yet he couldn't get total satisfaction; he had punished her mentally over a thousand times, yet her face came back always to haunt his dreams.

'Ay Poon,' he heard his mother calling.

'Yes Mother,' he answered.

'You fadder comin from by Ragbir now.'

'What must I do, Mother?'

'I nearly done cook. Soon you fadder goin to come and eat by de table. Now you have you head on, Poon. If you want dat money, you have to do as you modder say. Remember de plan we made up? Remember de brain you have in you head, you modder have it under she big toe. Oright.'

'Yes Mother.'

Poonwa got up from the bed. He went and made sure that the door was bolted from within. Peeping through the window, he had a glimpse of his father; Choonilal's head was bent as if he was worrying about something. Poonwa smiled and went back to the bed. He crushed the cigarette in the ashtray, and taking up the notebook again, he wrote:

| | |
|---|---|
| *Plane ticket* | $600.00 |
| *Suits* | $200.00 |
| *Grip and brief case* | $50.00 |
| *Shirts* | $50.00 |
| *Watch* | $200.00 |
| *Shoes* | $50.00 |
| *Camera* | $300.00 |

*Arriving in Canada with enough money to start my mission work.*

> *Poonwa of Karan Settlement,*
> *Missionary and philosopher.*
> *March 15, 1955.*

Poonwa took the notebook and studied what he had written. He was satisfied. He took the pencil and the notebook and put them back into the drawer of his desk.

Choonilal and Basdai were talking inside the kitchen.

Basdai said, 'You know dat we only have one chile, Choon. Don't be ungrateful to de boy. Remember how hard me and Pandit Puru had to pray befo Poon born. Say praise God dat you have a chile today.'

Choonilal softened a great deal, saying, 'Gal Bass, I willin to help de chile, but I cant just run and get rid of me property just like dat.'

'Well mortgage de property, boy Choon. Do it and help de chile, man.'

Striking his forehead with his palms, Choonilal maintained a stony silence.

Suddenly there was a scream from Poonwa's room.

'OOOOooooO! God! OOOO!'

Basdai ran into the hall. Grabbing a chair, putting it near the partition, climbing onto it, she peeped into Poonwa's room. Then she wailed, 'O God, Choon, you only chile dead in he room!'

The announcement of his son's death brought new life into Choonilal. He ran toward his son's door, but Basdai shouted, 'Go and call Pandit Puru!'

Choonilal hurried out on the junction and moaned, 'O God, Sook! Poonwa dead!'

'How he dead?'

But Choonilal had no time to waste. He bolted across the new road and headed for Ragbir's house.

Ragbir was in bed. He was fanning himself with his favourite blue towel. That towel meant a lot to him. It was given to him by an American general during the war. The Americans in their eagerness to defeat Germany had built a number of bases in Carib Island during the Second World War. There they sat in idleness most of the time during the day, then at night they used to invade the houses of the peasants and rape their daughters and kill their wives, and men who had the courage to oppose them were shot to death and thrown into the sea. They had a system of local spies headed by Ragbir who used to go into the village and pick out the beautiful women. At the end of the war, the American general gave Ragbir the blue towel he had wiped himself with after visits to the village women. Ragbir treasured the towel because it made him constantly remember those fun filled days with the Americans at Atkinson base.

Not expecting to leave his house just this minute, he was content to lie on his bed with the towel, wearing nothing but his old crotchless shorts which gave him freedom to scratch his testicles as he brooded over the generosity of the American general.

'Ay Ragbir!' Choonilal called from the road.

Ragbir sat up and asked, 'Wot happen boy Choon?'

'Poonwa dead, boy!'

'How he dead?'

'Me eh know.'

'Well hear nuh.'

But Choonilal had already crossed the new road.

Choonilal's announcement was too sudden; it interfered with Ragbir's mental equipment; it took him more than a minute of deep meditation to grasp the significance of Choonilal's message. But once he grasped it, the rest was easy. Wrapping his towel quickly around his head, he bolted out of the house in his crotchless shorts. As he ran, his enormous testicles bounced back and forth against his hairy legs, bounced and bounced as if they were trying to gain their independence.

When Ragbir reached the new road he couldn't cross right away. Cars were hurrying down to South City and hurrying up to Spanish City. He stood at the side of the road and cursed the drivers. Sweat came down from his head and made his neck sticky and uncomfortable. Some of the people in the cars were trying to give him a hard time; they were laughing and pointing at him. Unable to understand why they were so amused, Ragbir cursed and swore at them. From the roadside he heard the bawling that was going on at his friends' house. Then there was a fair enough gap between the cars. Ragbir ran over the road.

Tailor was in his room; he had been there since the quarrel examining the corridors of his mind. The corridors were empty, except for a few experiences that were lying here and there. One by one he examined them and smoked as he remembered the past. Suddenly the sound of Basdai's wailing sent him like lightning out of his room. He almost collided with Choonilal. There would have been a collision on the steps between Tailor and Choonilal, but Tailor, seeing the expression on Choonilal's face, shifted to one side. Then he went in the hall and began to wail with his landlady.

When Tailor ran upstairs he found Basdai screaming hysterically and pounding her head violently against her son's door. For a while Tailor wondered what to do. Now that Poonwa was dead, it meant that he would be able to live comfortably with the Choonilals. Tailor thought a little and decided not to weep. But as the prospect of homelessness came to him, he decided to weep, because by weeping he would be able to influence Basdai. Behaving as though Poonwa was his child, Tailor burst into tears. He was weeping and weeping, weeping more than Basdai even. Realizing that it was all going unobserved, he quickly embraced Basdai in a motherly fashion and pounded his head against the door. This new development had the desired effect. Basdai grabbed Tailor and said, 'O God, Tailor! You cryin too, Tail.'

Wishing to sustain Basdai's vision of the weeping tailor, he pounded his head with a savage determination. Each time that he drummed his head against the door he screamed. Sometimes he bent his head in such a way as to see his landlady's breasts as he wept. Now and then he abandoned the pounding of the door to strike his head against a softer material. Once or twice he struck his forehead against Basdai's breasts.

Sook and Rookmin were no amateurs when it came to weeping and getting on. From the time the queer reached upstairs and saw Tailor weeping and getting on, he decided to outdo the weeping tailor. Sook wept and started to butt the concrete wall. But the wall was too solid; there were a few small bruises on the queer's forehead on the first few encounters with the wall. Quickly switching his tactics, the queer moaned in baritone fashion. Each time that he wailed he butted away at the wooden chairs. There was Rookmin too, getting on as if Poonwa was her son. Wishing to do better than Sook, she stood with her legs wide apart and butted the wooden partition.

Ragbir was the last to reach. He stood for a moment and viewed the situation. He farted and slipped into the mood of the evening. Eager to kill two birds with one stone, he went down on the floor to weep. Gradually he crawled until he came by Rookmin. Then he slipped his head under her dress, and with his eyes to heaven he wept and wept.

This weeping went on for a long time until it began to get dark.

'Put on de lights,' Rookmin said.

Sook left the chairs alone and pulled the electric cord. There was light. As the lights came on, Rookmin jumped away from the partition. Ragbir got up from the floor and stood near Basdai. Tailor released his grasp from around Basdai's hips, and said to Rookmin, 'Look how Poon dead. He dead so easy. I was in me room, and me eh know wen he dead.'

And Basdai: 'If only Choon de listen to me, Poon wouda be livin now.'

It always distressed Sook when he heard about a young man's sudden departure. For a long time the queer had had his eyes on Poonwa. Poonwa was an intellectual and a philosopher. Sook had hoped that one day he would have an affair with Choonilal's intelligent son. The heart-broken queer cried out, 'O God! Poonwa de so yong. I tell you all dat boy, nuh. Well, he done dead, I might as well say it. I like de Poonwa so much.'

Basdai blinked her eyes when she heard Sook's confession. Sook had already led her husband into a number of homosexual affairs, and for a moment she felt like insulting him. But she controlled herself and said, 'Wot you go do boy Sook? Life is like dat.'

'It better dey de married de boy already,' Rookmin added.

Sook asked, 'How Poonwa dead?'

'He just bawl out and dead,' Basdai said quickly.

'All you see he dead, chile?' Ragbir asked.

Basdai winked a few times and said, 'He door lock.'

'Well break de door,' Tailor advised.

'Break it right now!' the queer commanded.

And Basdai: 'Dont touch dat door! Leff dat door till Pandit Puru reach in dis house.'

As Choonilal ran along the new road he felt guilt rising up and squeezing him. There were a few men strolling along the road casually. There were village women carrying tins of water on their heads. Many children dressed in rags were running on the pavement near Tola Hindu School. Some of the villagers approached Choonilal and tried to find out why he was crying as he ran along the road. But his mind was floating along with a heavy worry. It frightened him when he thought about his son's difficulties in the next life. Poonwa had been a believer in the Aryan gods. But he never did the sacrifices that were necessary to escape the Law of Karma. It grieved Choonilal that he couldn't foresee the rebirth of his son. Apart from the questions of immortality, there were the more practical questions. Through sun and rain Choonilal had laboured on the sugarcane plantations to get the money to support Poonwa in school. The weeping Choonilal was trying to get away from thinking about the mortgage business. He allowed his mind to run along all kinds of topics and incidents. At times he even smiled a little when his mind settled on his affairs with Sook, but even his experiences with the queer couldn't keep the remorse from welling up inside him. Guilt assaulted his feelings; he couldn't forgive himself for not signing the mortgage papers in time. When he reached by the entrance to the Hindu School he didn't bother to open the gate; he just jumped over it and ran toward the house of the priest.

Pandit Puru had begun life as a peasant. But now he lived in an aristocratic house just behind Tola Hindu School. As Choonilal approached him, he paid his respects to the holy man.

'Sita Ram Baba,' Choonilal said.

'Sita Ram beta,' Pandit Puru said.

The priest was decked out in a pair of cowboy boots. A fresh coat of polish made the boots shine, and the fancy brass buckles made them look elegant and expensive. Sitting on an expensive cushion in his yard, the holy man sipped a glass of chilled whisky as his brown eyes scanned the sunset. He was in a meditative mood: his brow was slightly furrowed, his eyes were pensive, and his black whiskers were conspicuous, a ball of green snot hanging from the hairs.

'Wot happen?' the priest asked, his eyes still following the tired sun

'Poonwa dead.'

The priest jerked his head. The green ball fell from his whiskers and stuck to the chest of his white gown. 'How he dead?'

'I dont know. But he dead.'

'You should glad,' Pandit Puru said. He took a sip of whisky and continued. 'If you de give dat boy de money, he wouda live. You is a nasty man.'

Choonilal wanted to speak up and give the reasons why he had been afraid to sign the mortgage papers. In 1950 Pandit Puru had a vision: one of the Aryan gods told him that the Hindus in Carib Island needed a great temple. The idea was preached to the peasants. Then Pandit Puru formed a committee. He used his influence and had all his sons elected into executive offices. Then he organized a raffle. More than five hundred thousand books of tickets were sold in Carib Island; Choonilal alone bought fifty books, he had paid the fifty dollars for them willingly. Then the rest of the tickets were taken to Trinidad and sold on the Sugar Belt to the Hindus; the remaining books were sold in Guyana. It had been made known in the West Indies that Tola was going to have the greatest Hindu temple; local architects were not competent; they were unholy; architects were to be brought from India. So Pandit Puru sent his sons to India to look for religious architects. Once they were in India they enrolled in Indian universities and began studying medicine with the money they had collected for the temple. Then Pandit Puru bought a few expensive motor cars, built a spacious house, installed two telephones, hired a few household servants, a chauffeur, a messenger boy, and married off his daughters to fat rich Brahmins in Spanish City and South City, then he settled down to enjoy his luxuries. Choonilal couldn't bring this up, because his son was dead; he needed the priest to perform the death ceremony. So he said softly, 'I didn't know de chile wouda dead, Baba.'

'My ass you didnt know!' Pandit Puru shouted. Then in a softer voice he asked, 'How much money you goin to pay me to do de ceremony?'

Choonilal batted his eyes saying, 'Ten dollars, Baba.'

'Fifty.'

Choonilal met him halfway. 'Twenty-five.'

'Fifty dollars, or get out of me yard.'

'Oright, Baba, fifty dollars,' Choonilal said.

Beads of perspiration formed on the priest's forehead. He tapped his head as if to drive away some unpleasant thoughts. Rubbing his soft hands together, he muttered, 'If you de sign de blasted mortgage, it wouda be oright.'

'Let we go now, Baba,' Choonilal said, with a certain tightness in his voice.

Pandit Puru looked insulted. 'Karan Settlement a half-mile away from dis place. Just now wen me chauffeur come wid de car, I go go wid you.'

Choonilal felt like screaming at the priest. In days gone by, Pandit Puru had walked barefoot all over the village like a mendicant. He used to walk for miles and miles to perform a death ceremony. But Choonilal said nothing; Pandit Puru was the representative of the gods on earth.

A little later a Cadillac pulled into the yard. The holy man whispered something to the thin Indian chauffeur. The driver looked at Choonilal and said, 'Siddown in de back.'

'Oright.'

The priest sat in front and belched continuously.

As they rode along, Choonilal thought of all the bad things he had done to his son.

Choonilal had a two-storeyed house. It took him thirty years to save the money to build it. The house stood on ten-foot concrete pillars. The house was modern and spacious, with three bedrooms, a lovely verandah, a large hall, a modern kitchen equipped with a gas stove and three aluminum sinks. There was a cabinet with expensive chinaware which the Choonilals never used, except on special occasions; there were wooden cupboards in which the groceries were kept; next to the stove was a large fridge which they kept only for the purpose of making ice cubes, since as Hindus they were not supposed to put meat into the freezer. There was also a modern bathroom. In the bathroom there was a medicine cabinet. The toilet was something evil for Choonilal and Basdai; it was used only by Poonwa. Choonilal and Basdai felt that a toilet was a threat to them; especially Choonilal, he believed it was irreligious to empty his bowels inside his own house.

When Choonilal had first thought about a house, he had never thought about the possibility of putting a toilet upstairs. He had always looked upon those Hindus who used modern toilets as sacreligious people. About two years ago, when the carpenter had informed Choonilal that there was going to be a modern bathroom upstairs, he had been so mad that he had run the carpenter out of his yard with a machete. He believed that the Aryan gods were going to hate him for the rest of his life. He had a feeling too that they were going to doom him to a cycle of rebirths after death. Basdai agreed with Choonalil: a latrine was a threat to the gods. But when Poonwa came from work that evening and heard that his father had had the courage to chase the carpenter away, he got mad. Poonwa was a Hindu, but he was a modern Hindu. He had been emptying his bowels all his life in outhouses. But with the job as a lawyer clerk in Spanish City, he had known the good fortune to discover the wonders of a modern toilet. His employer's toilet had exercised a special attraction for him. There were no smells; there were no flies; there was always that soft seat and the rolls of tissue paper; there was that special kind of security, which created an atmosphere of pleasantness: it was so pleasant that Poonwa used to eat his lunch while he defecated.

So when Poonwa heard what his father had done to the carpenter, he said that a toilet upstairs was a necessity. To Choonilal this was high-class heresy. He stated vehemently that he wasn't going to have a toilet upstairs. For a moment it looked as if father and son were going to have a fight; but Choonilal was too coward to allow this kind of development. Then Poonwa threatened that he was going to leave Karan Settlement and live in Spanish City. Choonilal knew that Spanish City was not a safe place for a Hindu boy to live; it was only a good place for a Hindu to work. The city was too dangerous: there were stabbings in the alleyways and whores plied their trade on dark street corners. So the next day Choonilal went and begged the carpenter to continue with the toilet project. The carpenter was puzzled; just the day before Choonilal had chased him with a cutlass; today he was begging him to build the washroom upstairs. When the carpenter had inquired why Choonilal had changed so quickly, he had frightened the carpenter with a deadly silence.

As the toilet incident rushed through Choonilal's mind, the feeling of remorse came back to trouble him. Feeling that he couldn't keep it any more to himself, he said to Pandit Puru, 'Baba, you know dat I de get on wid Poonwa, wen he de want de latrine upstairs.'

'You is a nasty man,' the priest said. 'If you de sign dat mortgage paper, Poonwa wouda be still livin. But you like to keep all wot you have for youself.'

Choonilal wanted to ask the holy man about the money for the temple and remind him how his sons had gone to India to look for ascetic architects but had settled for degrees in Indian universities instead. But he said nothing. He just sat and stared at the bald head of the chauffeur, wondering how the driver had lost his hair.

When the car pulled up near the house, Sook, Rookmin, and Ragbir came out on the verandah. They were still sobbing a little. Choonilal and the priest came out of the car, but the chauffeur sat behind the wheel. As the priest ascended the steps, Ragbir said, 'Wot happening, Baba?'

In days gone by the priest would have answered, 'Notten at all, man Ragbir man.' But since he had got rich he had no time for this kind of talk. As if locked in thought, Pandit Puru walked into the hall with pursed lips. He said to the weeping Basdai, 'Wot happen, beti?'

Basdai didn't tell him anything about Poonwa; it was as if he hadn't asked a question. She just said, 'Come in de kitchen. I want to talk to you alone, Baba.'

They went into the kitchen. Then the priest ran out and said, 'Let all de people go downstairs!'

'Wot happen, Baba?' Choonilal asked in a terrified voice.

'Just tell dem to go downstairs!'

'Oright, Baba.'

'All you go downstairs,' Choonilal said to his neighbours.

Sook said, 'But how you coud tell we dat, Choon? All de time we cryin upstairs and now you tellin we to go downstairs.'

'Is Baba who say to send all you below. Not me.'

Sook, Rookmin, Ragbir, and Tailor went downstairs.

The priest batted his eyes, then took out a large volume of the *Bhagavad Gita*. He read a little, then he said to Choonilal, 'You son not dead, Choon.'

'How you know dat, Baba?'

'De *Bhagavad Gita* say dat.'

'So he still livin in de room?'

'Yeh, beta.'

'Den I want to talk to him, Baba,' Choonilal said anxiously.

Pandit Puru batted his eyes again and said, 'You cant talk to him, Choon.'

'But why, Baba?'

'Because he had a vision from God.'

'Wot de vision was about, Baba?'

'About de Hindu Mission to Canada,' the priest said.

'Wot!' Choonilal shouted.

'Dont bawl like dat at Baba. It not good to bawl at de Pandit,' Basdai warned.

'I not kiss-me-ass bawlin!' Choonilal shouted.

'You want people to hear you business in de road?' Basdai asked hotly.

'De people coud hear wot de modderass dey like!' Choonilal screamed.

'If you bawl like dat again, I go make de gods give you trobble till you cant take,' Pandit Puru said.

This talk about the gods floated on Choonilal's mind, floated and floated until it settled at the bottom of his consciousness. It was a serious matter. Remembering how he had neglected the gods, Choonilal said, 'Is oright, Baba. I sorry.'

'Try and behave youself,' the priest said.

'Oright, Baba.'

Then the priest told Choonilal to go downstairs and call the people. When he reached downstairs Sook asked him, 'Wot happen, Choon? I hear you mout hard hard just now, man.'

'Poonwa not dead.'

'Wot!' they shouted as if with one voice.

'You mean we was cryin all de time in vain?' Rookmin asked.

'Yeh,' Choonilal said.

Ragbir knitted his brows and said, 'Wot de happen to Poonwa?'

'He de have a vision or someting like dat. Dat is wot de Pandit say.'

'Well I goin to tell you something, Choon, dat Pandit playin he ass! Choon, as I see it, dat priest playin a game for your property. Believe me, boy.'

Tailor spoke up: 'Choonilal, dont worry wid Ragbir. If Baba say dat Poonwa see a God, den he see a God. Pandit not goin to lie. He is a priest. Remember dat.'

'Tailor, look here, shut you kiss-me-ass mout,' Ragbir said. 'Dis house and land is Choon own. He work hard to make it. If I was Choon, I wouda done run you ass outa Karan Settlement.'

The queer said smoothly, 'Tailor and Ragbir, all you wrong to talk like dat. Choon is a big man, he know wot to do. If all you advise him, all you go get a bad name in the de end.'

'Dat is true,' Ragbir declared.

And now that he was upstairs with his neighbours, Choonilal was greatly agitated. Poonwa and Pandit Puru were sitting on the couch. When Choonilal saw his son, he jerked his head as if Poonwa was a ghost.

'Sit down, Father,' Poonwa said coldly.

Choonilal sat on a chair. He was trembling. There was a coat of sweat on his bald head. He clutched the ends of the chair, because his hands were trembling too much.

Ragbir, Tailor, Rookmin, and Sook remained standing.

'Now,' Pandit Puru said.

Choonilal jumped up. 'Wot, Baba?'

'God appear to you son and tell him dat he have to go on dat Mission. Now remember dat is not a man who appear to him. Just remember dat. Now de way I see it is like dis. You very lucky to have a son like Poonwa in de fust place. For God to talk to you son, you have to be a great man. Now you have to sign dat mortgage papers and send dis boy to Canada.'

'But sappose I dont sign de mortgage, Baba?'

'Den Poonwa goin to remain in Karan Settlement,' the priest said.

'Well den he go have to remain home,' Choonilal said shakily.

The priest scratched his testicles a little, thought a little, then said, 'De Hindu gods go make you see trobble till you shit, Choonilal!'

Choonilal almost fell off his chair. That was a serious threat.

Rookmin felt it was her turn to say something. She faked a little cough and said, 'Choon, you shoud send Poonwa. Carib Island have no future for de boy. Send him over, man. All de future he have on dis island is to come a police or a postman or a teacher, den drink drink rum till he dead.'

'You better shut you mout, woman,' the queer said.

'You better shut you ass, Sook!' Rookmin shouted.

Basdai had been sitting quietly all the time. She said, 'I want Poonwa to go over. Let he fadder make up he mind to sign dem papers tomorrow, else it goin to have trobble in dis house.'

'Oright! Oright!' Pandit Puru screamed. 'Let de chile say wot de vision was about.'

There was silence. Poonwa said that he had gone to his room to try to get some sleep. But he couldn't sleep; he was hearing a flute playing the sacred flute that Krishna had played to the milkmaids. The music was enchanting. He listened and listened until he reached a stage of bliss. Then Lord Krishna appeared to him and told him that he was going to become a great Hindu missionary in North America. After Krishna blessed him, the god vanished.

'Why you didnt come outta you room wen all dat noise was goin on?' Ragbir asked.

Poonwa refused to answer.

Pandit Puru thought a little, then he began to sing some hymns. This made the people quiet.

Then the priest stopped suddenly. He said to Choonilal, 'If God command you, you go disobey?'

Before Choonilal could answer, Pandit Puru began another hymn.

Then Poonwa threw himself on the floor.

'Run and get a soda water!' the priest shouted at Sook.

But Sook had no intentions of going for soda water. He said to his wife, 'You go for de soda water nuh.'

As soon as Rookmin left, the queer said, 'Come downstairs wid me, Rag, I want to tell you someting.'

When they were downstairs, the queer held on to Ragbir's balls, which still hung from his crotchless shorts. 'O God, Rag, you have to bull me tonight.'

It was only when Sook held his organ that Ragbir realized he had worn his old shorts to go to Choonilal's house. Everybody had seen him. He ran toward his house. But Sook was excited; he wasn't going to allow a golden opportunity to slip by. Sook ran behind Ragbir and followed him into his house.

❖

Like her husband, Basdai had always taken the gods seriously. Her marriage had been saved as a result of their direct intervention into her life. When she had married Choonilal thirty years ago, she was prepared to live the life of a devoted Hindu partner; she was prepared to bear Choonilal a brood of sons and daughters, because a childless marriage is a misfortune to all Hindu couples. And when she came to Karan Settlement she knew that she was going to have many children; that was the reason why after the first week of her marriage she had taken a cutlass and worked with her husband side by side on the sugar plantation. Her ability to work had made Choonilal happy. In those days too, Basdai was very thin – a good sign, because thin women are better child bearers. In his mind Choonilal knew that in days to come he would establish his own dynasty in Karan Settlement. But as the months went by, Choonilal had had a feeling of insecurity. He had been giving his wife her share every night in bed. Yet there were no signs of pregnancy.

Then something else happened. Basdai began to grow fat and Choonilal began to get thinner. During the first few weeks of their marriage Choonilal used to give Basdai jokes about her size. Then a few months later it became Basdai's turn to give the jokes. This went on until the day the process seemed to have ended. Basdai remained fleshy and her husband was stuck with the skinny look. In those days Choonilal had prayed and prayed to the gods to reverse the process, because he wanted a thin wife. But the gods hadn't the time to change back the whole process.

And when they had been married, Basdai had a thin reddish kind of hair; Choonilal had always feared that his wife would grow bald one day. But a few months after they were married, nature took care of that problem in an easy way. Suddenly Basdai's hair began to get thick and black. After a while she had very good hair. Then something happened: Choonilal went bald, and his skull took on a reddish appearance. He hadn't the courage to face the facts of his hairlessness. He used to burst into maddening rages and flog his wife all over the village. Choonilal would bite her at night, and sometimes when he was drunk enough he used to hold on to her hair and drag her all over the house. Then one day he sat under the chataigne tree and decided that he couldn't live with his wife any more. During the course of that night, he made up his mind that at daybreak he was going to send back his wife to her parents in Bhagi Tola. But during that night Hanuman the monkey god had the audacity to invade Choonilal's brain. He dreamt that Hanuman threatened to kill him if ever he sent Basdai away.

That was a long time ago. As Choonilal remembered the dream, he turned to Basdai on the bed and said with a certain amount of sadness and regrets, 'Gal Bass, God is good yeh.'

Almost immediately after Choonilal opened his mouth, he realized that he had said the wrong thing. For Basdai said, 'Dat is de reason why you have to send Poonwa on dat mission to Canada.'

After the priest left, Choonilal was so worried that he had a restless night. Pandit Puru had told Choonilal that he was going to come with the lawyer today. Although Choonilal had not said anything, he had known that Pandit Puru would come. This made him so sad all night that he had not closed his eyes for a single minute. All night he heard his son snoring in the next room, and mentally he had murdered Poonwa about fifty times before daybreak. He hadn't only murdered Poonwa; he had murdered Basdai also, murdered her about one hundred times. Perhaps he would have slept; there were times when his eyes were burning, and his nose was itching, and his ears were ringing, and he knew that it was the sign that he was going to fall asleep. But he couldn't fall asleep. There had been a snoring competition all night between his wife and his son, and toward dawn his wife won. All night too, Tailor had been coughing and breaking wind downstairs and stand-ing on the steps and urinating in the yard. Once or twice he thought he heard Sook's voice downstairs and he knew that the queer and Tailor were having an affair. And a few times Choonilal actually attempted to get out of bed to start a row with his tenant, but he remained in bed; he wanted to save his energy for the encounter with the priest.

'You goin to send dat boy on de Hindu Mission to Canada or not, Choon? Make up you mind. Today is de day.'

'I didnt sleep whole night last night,' Choonilal said.

'Look, Choon, dont play in you ass! I talkin about cow and you talkin about dog. I ask you if you make up you mind to send Poonwa on dat Mission.'

Choonilal yawned and said, 'Tink how hard we work to make dis house and land wot it is today. You dont tink dat Poonwa coud stay in de island? Wen we dead, he go have he house and land. Wot else he want? Bass, you know dat Pandit Puru make all dat ruction about de Hindu temple. Den he take de money and he send he son and dem to study in India. Sappose he tief away de house and land wen we sign dat paper?'

It was a reasonable question, but Basdai was not in a reasonable mood. She grabbed Choonilal's testicles and said, 'Is he son and dem who tief de money and gone to India! You hear dat!'

'Yeh! Yeh!' Choonilal screamed.

When Basdai released him, Choonilal groaned for a while.

The sun was bright and rising fast in the sky. The light penetrated the glass window and fell upon Choonilal and Basdai. Basdai felt good as the light rays danced over her body, this was because she had snored all night. But Choonilal couldn't take the rays. A kind of giddiness came into his head. Then he sneezed about ten times. Water was flowing from his red eyeballs. 'Pull de curtain nuh, gal Bass,' he said

'Wot you want?'

'Pull de curtain nuh.'

'Wot happen? Like de sun go eat you?'

'No gal. Me head hurtin me bad bad.'

'I not doin notten for you till you sign dat mortgage papers!'

Choonilal remained on the bed. Long ago he would have settled the matter quite easily. Whenever Basdai had been grouchy in the past, it was no problem. He used to hold her and give her a few hard whacks on her backside, and that made her obey him. But he knew that he couldn't try that kind of a thing this morning. Twenty years ago, if Basdai had supported a Hindu Mission to Canada, Choonilal would have killed her. Unable to contemplate his helplessness, he said to her, 'You is me wife or you is not me wife?'

'I is notten to you, you dog. Notten to you till you sign dat mortgage.'

Choonilal felt like kicking her; in fact, his feet did stir a little, but he couldn't do that. He was content to lie in bed and look at the ceiling. But he couldn't stare at the ceiling for long. He had really begun staring there with the hope of finding some kind of solution to his household problems. But he couldn't think. Besides something was going wrong. Once or twice he thought he saw one of the Aryan gods laughing at him from the ceiling. This made his heart beat faster. When he looked up again he saw that it was a knot in the board. This settled him. Then out of curiosity he decided to look at the ceiling again; the knot turned again into a god. Choonilal shuddered and brought his eyes to rest upon something more earthly. He decided to look at the partition boards: they were painted in blue. He felt relaxed; Lord Krishna who had intoxicated Arjuna with sagelike wisdom was a blue god. Choonilal closed his eyes and meditated on blue. It was hard to meditate; Poonwa was snoring like an animal in the next room.

'I not sendin dat son of a bitch on no mission!' Choonilal shouted.

Then a stench began to come into the house. All night the outhouse had been giving out fumes, but over a period of two months Choonilal had recorded minutely the different levels of scent. This morning it smelt worst than ever. Choonilal wanted to curse Tailor, but he felt too weak to start a quarrel. Then he thought that the smell was perhaps only inside his head. This made him tremble.

'You smellin someting?' Basdai asked.

With a feeling of relief he said, 'Yeh.'

'See wot it is.'

'Oright.'

Choonilal peeped through the window. He pulled back in his head quickly and smiled.

'Wot de ass you doin you mout so for?'

'Tailor cleanin de latrine. Ragbir helpin him too,' Choonilal said.

Then there was a little silence that ended with Basdai saying, 'You givin Poonwa dat money?'

'Let Poonwa kiss me ass! I sorry dat boy born.'

This wasn't a good thing to say. Years after they had been married they couldn't have a child. Those were the days when Choonilal used to pray and beg the gods for a child. After three years Choonilal had realized that the gods were playing the fool; he was functioning well, yet Basdai couldn't have a child. For a while Choonilal had abandoned the gods. One day he had told his wife that doctors were their only hope. Basdai had agreed. Choonilal took her down to Spanish City to consult an English doctor; he had no confidence in Indian and Negro doctors. When the doctor heard Basdai complain, he said that she had nothing to worry about. He gave her some yellow tablets and told her to take one a day. Basdai took a tablet the next morning; she defecated green. She panicked. Her husband had great confidence in the white doctor; he calmed her down. She took another yellow tablet the next day. This time she defecated black. Choonilal panicked. He ordered her to throw away the tablets. But the tablets were very expensive. She took another one. When she defecated black again, Choonilal flung the tablets into the latrine pit.

For a while they had waited and watched. Two months went by. Still there were no signs of pregnancy. As the prospect of childlessness gazed at the Choonilals, they developed the doctor mania again. They went to the white doctor and complained. He apologized and gave them some white tablets; Basdai urinated pink the next day. They went back and told the doctor that they didn't believe in tablets; Sook had told them that injections were better. But the doctor had some kind of massaging business to do before he gave the injections. Choonilal was told to wait outside; Basdai was commanded to undress, an activity that took some time, because in those days Basdai always went out with a sari. With his delicate fingers the doctor massaged her bottom and then injected her. Basdai was always uneasy; she couldn't adapt to the idea of pink hands massaging her dark backside. As the weeks went by the doctor became more aggressive. One day, whether by chance or by purpose (the intention was never established), the doctor slipped his fingers up her two holes. She screamed. Choonilal pushed open the little door but hadn't asked a question; the doctor glanced at him ferociously. In order to keep Basdai's character intact, the Choonilals never spoke of this incident. It was Ragbir who had picked it up somewhere and brought it as a scandal to Karan Settlement.

In those days Choonilal had had a great feeling to sue the doctor, but the thought of policemen and jail and the loss of character for his wife pacified him. When the white doctor failed, for Choonilal it meant that all white doctors were no good. He took his wife to a Negro specialist. There was no hope; the Negro took too much liberty on the subject of sex; he used to give long lectures, but the Choonilals did not understand them. Basdai got fed up with the doctor on her first visit. But Choonilal decided to patronize the doctor for a while. He knew the Negro was no good, but the Negro spoke good English, better than a white man, in Choonilal's opinion. During each visit the doctor used to tell Basdai about 'positions,' tell her how to move her hips and how not to move her hips. One day when he said to her that if she tried it from behind it was going to help, Basdai ran out of the office.

The doctor-mania ended, but the Pandit-mania began. Choonilal and Basdai consulted Pandit Puru. He told them about the peace and serenity of cohabiting outdoors. They tried it. They stuck like dogs. After that scandal Choonilal lost his taste for women with an astonishing swiftness. Suspending his love for Basdai, he formed a liaison with Sook. Sodomy had its charms; for a while it looked as if Choonilal might take Sook away from Rookmin. But Basdai didn't lose hope. Every night she and Pandit Puru used to pray inside the house. It was never known in what position they prayed, but Basdai became pregnant. When Choonilal learnt of her pregnancy, he abandoned the queer and went back to his wife. Choonilal believed that it was prayers that made his wife pregnant. While Poonwa was small, Choonilal thought he was the son of one of the Aryan gods; after all, Hanuman the monkey god was a bastard. Day and night Choonilal used to keep his eyes on Poonwa; he had a feeling that one day his son was going to turn into a bird and fly away, or turn into a monkey and live in the bushes, or just disappear altogether. But as the years passed and Choonilal didn't notice any godly transformations in Poonwa, he accepted the belief that Basdai's child was just the son of man.

Basdai turned on the bed and said, 'You is a ungrateful man, Choon.'
'How I ungrateful?'

'You used to pray to God to have a chile. Wen Poonwa de born you de say dat you go give you life for him. Today you makin trobble about de money to send him on de Hindu Mission.'

'Wot de ass he want to go on mission pission for?'

'He just want to teach white people about Hinduism, Choon.'

'Well, lemme tell you someting, woman,' Choonilal said, 'and you lissen good. White people woudnt even pee on Poonwa. You hear dat. You tink dat white people is like Indian and Creole? Well if you tink so, you makin a mistake. White people make Creole pull cart in slavery yeh. You tink is joke.'

'But Poonwa say dat just how white people come here and teach we about Jesus Christ and ting, just so he go teach dem about Rama and Krishna.'

'You tink white people want to read Indian books?' Choonilal asked.

'Well, Poonwa say he goin to open a school and teach dem to read in Hindi. I tink he coud do it. How dem white people who come on dat Canadian Mission to Carib Island beat dem Indians and make dem learn English? How come dey make de Indians Christians? Well de same way Poonwa goin to beat dey ass and make dem learn Hindi. I tink he coud do it.'

'He go do it wen cock get teets,' Choonilal said.

'You mean dat white people so bad dat dey eh go allow him to open he school and ting?'

And Choonilal: 'You dont know wot white people give, nuh. Dey want dis whole world for deyself, yeh. Poonwa only foolin around … '

Poonwa shouted from the next room, 'Father, why don't you shut up! Shut up! Just shut up!'

Choonilal trembled. Basdai jumped out of bed saying, 'I goin to cook, because it lookin late like hell.'

At daybreak Tailor was on the move; he woke with the intention to clean the pit. Going to the outhouse, he examined the excreta and worms, spat a few times, cursed a little, and went back under the house.

Making a mental note of all the things he needed, he went over to the rum shop. He stood on the road and called Sook. There was no answer. He called again. This time the northern bedroom window opened and the queer peeped out. 'What you want, Tail?'

'I want to get some tings from de shop man, Sook.'

'I comin now.'

Sook hurried downstairs. Opening one of the wooden doors, he said, 'Come in.'

When Tailor was inside, the queer bolted the door. 'How you get up so early, Tail?'

'I get up soon to clean de pit man Sook.'

'Choon and dem get up aready?'

Tailor scratched his head. 'Last night whole night Choon coughin and fartin, man. I didnt get no sleep. Dat mission ting worryin him too bad. Wost again, Pandit Puru comin today wid dat lawyer.'

'Wot you want from de shop?' the queer asked briskly.

Tailor said he wanted an enamel bucket, a pound of goat's rope, and a pair of rubber boots.

Placing the items on the counter, Sook said, 'Twenty dollars.'

'Mark it on Choonilal account. It is he latrine.'

'I cant do dat.'

'Why?'

The shopkeeper complained that Choonilal hadn't paid him in a long time.

Remembering that Basdai bought most of her groceries in Tolaville, he said, 'I feel you lyin, Sook.'

'I dont have to lie for you, Tail.'

But Tailor had to come to some kind of agreement because Rookmin had stopped him from using Sook's pit and he had a feeling that Choonilal was going to quarrel about the pit today again. He was scared. His landlord was growing more nervous every day. Tailor's own conscience was eating him as well. He had caused Basdai to empty her bowels at midnight in the sugarcane field. Then Choonilal had to use Ragbir's pit, and Tailor had to use Sook's outhouse. 'Well, Sook, gimme dese tings on credit. Wen I sew some cloes I go pay you. Oright.'

'I cant give you no credit.'

'But next week I gettin some cloes to sew,' Tailor told him. 'Wen de people pay me, I go run over de road and pay you, man. Dont worry about de money. You money good like gold, man Sook.'

The shopkeeper wasn't going to fall for that; he knew too much about Tailor and his sewing activities. He remembered the time when Choonilal had bought the electric sewing machine for Tailor. It was around Carnival time; the villagers were glad to give their clothes to the tailor in Karan Settlement. Some Negro boys up in Lima Road had organized a little band to play mass in Tolaville. They bought some pattern books and some expensive cloth and came to Tailor. The boys wanted the costumes sewed in a particular way. Tailor said that that was no trouble; he took an advance and told the boys to collect their clothes on the following weekend. Tailor burnt his landlord's current day and night, and Choonilal didn't mind; he wanted to see Tailor make some money. When Basdai complained about the constant purring of the machine day and night, Choonilal told her that she had to tolerate the sound only for a few days. When weekend came around and the Negroes saw what the Indian tailor had done with their expensive clothes, they pulled Tailor out of his little room and started beating him in Choonilal's yard. The beating would have continued, because Choonilal was too scared to come to Tailor's rescue that time, but Ragbir took a cutlass and ran over the new road as a madman.

'Wot you goin to do? You goin to give me dese tings?' Tailor asked.

'I not doin dat, boy,' Sook said.

'Oright,' Tailor said as he turned to go out.

'Tailor, remember you does shit in me latrine.'

'Yeh.'

'I ever charge you money for dat?'

'No.'

'Well if you bull me, I go give you dese tings you come to buy free.'

'But I bull you last night, Sook, after you done get your bullin by Rag.'

'Dat was last night. But you have to bull me dis mornin to get dese tings free.'

'Oright,' Tailor said.

While Sook was unbuttoning his trouser with one hand, he opened the fridge with the other, took out a stout, uncapped it, and handing it to Tailor he said, 'Drink dat fust. It go make you strong like a lion.'

Ragbir too had had a restless night. The Aryan gods were constantly invading his sleep and running him all over the village. He was sitting by his window and fanning himself with his favourite blue towel. Every day Choonilal used to come to use his outhouse. Ragbir was hoping to see Choonilal. During the night he had thought a lot about Poonwa's Hindu Mission to Canada. It was clear to him that Pandit Puru was behind the Mission because he wanted to steal Choonilal's property. And Tailor was supporting the Mission because he wanted to have a grip on the Choonilals. The outhouse door was open; Ragbir leaned over the window and looked. There was no one in it. Ragbir wondered why Choonilal hadn't come as yet to defecate. He cursed Choonilal. Then he began to concentrate on the road. Every morning at daybreak Poonwa used to stand on the junction with his right hand sticking out. He couldn't afford to take a taxi or the bus to work; he was working for too little. But Poonwa was not on the junction. Yesterday Ragbir had heard something about Poonwa leaving the job in the city; but he hadn't heard all. As he stared at the junction he realized that the rumour was true. He cursed himself for not asking Choonilal about it yesterday. But he couldn't get the chance to ask Choonilal about it yesterday; too much had turned too suddenly. Ragbir sat there and hoped that Choonilal would come to defecate in his pit, but his neighbour was not showing up. Basdai too had been an early bird always. Long before daybreak Ragbir used to see her moving in the kitchen. Last night all the lights had been on in Choonilal's house, and at times Ragbir had seen people moving in the house. But he felt that he had dreamt that. Eager to hear about what went on in his neighbour's last night, Ragbir tied the blue towel around his head and crossed the new road.

'Wot you doin boy Tail?'

'I just plannin to clean de pit, man Rag.'

'So you make up you mind at last?'

'Yeh man Rag. De damn latrine does stink too bad man. Choonilal is a lazy bugger. He don't want to help me to clean de damn ting.'

Tailor was sitting under the chataigne tree with the bucket, the rope, and the pair of rubber boots. His crotch was open. Ragbir laughed and said, 'Button you crotch nuh man Tail. It too early to have you ting hangin out like dat man.'

Tailor buttoned up his pants.

'But how you ting hangin out so early man?' Ragbir asked.

'Wen I get up I de forget to button me pants man Rag.'

'And which part you get dat bucket and ting?'

'I de buy dese tings since two three weeks ago man Rag.'

But Ragbir had seen when the village tailor had gone over by Sook. At first he had thought that Tailor had gone to defecate by Sook. Then he knew that Tailor had gone to do some kind of business, for he saw when Tailor came out of the shop with the bucket, the rope, and the rubber boots. Ragbir pointed a finger at Tailor. 'You cant fool me, Tail. You bull Sook. We men dont have to hide notten. If you bull Sook you bull him. Dat is all.'

'Oright,' Tailor said, 'I bull him dis mornin.'

Ragbir laughed and said, 'You is a nasty man, Tailor!'

'How?'

'So much women in de village and you bullin man. Befo you ride Sook, you shouda ride Basdai.'

Tailor didn't want to talk about Basdai with Ragbir, so he asked, 'You ever bull Sook, Rag?'

Ragbir wiped his bearded mouth with the back of his hand. 'You tink I go leave women to ride man. You must be tink dat I born by me modder backside.'

Then they settled down to more serious business. 'I come to help you clean de pit man,' Ragbir said.

This caused Tailor to jerk his head a little; Ragbir was a lazy man; he had been lazy all his life. 'Like you get up in a hard-workin mood?'

'I come to help you and so you go talk,' Ragbir said.

They went by the outhouse with the bucket, the rope, and the rubber boots. The pit was stinking.

'Go and get some cotton to put in we nose,' Ragbir said.

Tailor got the cotton. They stuffed up their noses. 'You clean fust. I go bail after,' Ragbir said.

'But de odder hole not dig yet,' Tailor observed.

'Well dig it.'

'Oright.'

Tailor took a fork and dug a hole. Then he removed the old wooden seat and started to empty the contents of the pit into the new hole.

Ragbir had no intentions of helping Tailor. Last night after he had left Choonilal's house in his crotchless shorts, he had gone to his own house with the thought of coming back in a while. But Sook had followed him; when the affair was over, Ragbir couldn't go back, because he had to meet Basdai in the trace. As Tailor was emptying the pit Ragbir asked, 'How everybody so quiet in de house?'

Tailor talked as he worked. 'Man wot I go tell you, Rag. Last night whole night I hear Choon turnin in he bed. He and Basdai de quarrellin now and den. One time last night Poon was gettin on wid he fadder about dat Mission to Canada. One time in de night Choon de bawlin hard hard. At fust I de tink dat he de ridin Basdai. But it de look to me like she de squeezin he stones. Last night Basdai didnt go and shit in dat cane. Lemme tell you someting. Basdai look like she shit last night in de toilet upstairs.'

Ragbir looked worried. Since Basdai had started doing her toilet in the canefield, Ragbir would seduce her in the trace. Last night after his affair with Sook he had gone to the trace to meet her. He waited for a few hours and when she didn't show up returned home very upset.

'You sure she shit upstairs?' he asked Tailor.

'Yeh man Rag, Poon alone cant leggo leer all de time.'

This was bad news; Ragbir had been planning to seduce Basdai in the sugarcane field. 'Basdai is a modderass den,' he said more to himself than to his listener.

The listener asked, 'Why?'

But Ragbir didn't bother to say any more about the plans he had had for Basdai. He just said, 'Wot you tink about Poon Mission to Canada? Tell me de truth, boy Tail.'

'I tink it is a good ting, yeh. After all, white people come here and teach we English and ting, now is time for we to teach dem we language. Dat is only fair. But it too much look to me like Poon want a man in he ass.'

And Ragbir: 'As I see it, Poon want about five six man in he ass. If somebody hold Poon and bull him, he go forget all dat Mission talk. Poon want a good man, and like Choon blind. If Choon wasnt me friend I wouda hold Poon and leggo some totey on him yeh. No joke nuh.'

'But I tink you tell me dat you dont like man. Wot happen so suddenly?'

Worms were running all over the place; they were trying to climb up on Tailor's rubber boots. Ragbir moved away a little. 'Man Rag, like dese worms want man in dey ass.'

'Well bull dem, nuh,' Ragbir declared.

The stench from the pit was almost unbearable. 'People shit is de wost kinda shit to smell,' Tailor said. 'Cow shit does smell nice. Horse shit does smell good too. Goat shit and sheep shit is nice shit to smell. But dog shit does stink like people own, you know boy Rag.'

'Korek.'

'You know wen I de small boy Rag, we de have a goat. Wen I de small man sometime I used to eat goat shit man Rag.'

'Wot make you stop?'

Realizing that he had said something about his past life, Tailor maintained a stony silence.

Poonwa was lying down on his bed and smoking a cigarette. Last night he had slept well, but his dreams were nightmares. He had dreamt that he was a little boy, a pupil at the Canadian Mission School in Tolaville. There was the white school mistress, but in the dream she was white only from the face to the hips; she was black underneath, and her feet was not human feet, they were large hooves. He was sitting at the back of the class and trying to learn the alphabet. Everything was all right. Then the teacher came to the back of the class; it was then that he discovered she was black from the hips down. At one time she was choking him in the punishment room in the school; at another moment she was running him like a horse and trying to trample him on the streets in Tolaville. Then she caught him and dragged him into the school's outhouse. She gave him food and told him to eat. As he bit the food she held his chest and squeezed him down on the ground; she was squeezing hard; he wanted to bawl, but he couldn't. This kind of dream had occurred many nights before; there was hardly a night when Poonwa didn't dream that school mistress in some form or the other. Putting out the cigarette in the ashtray, he pulled the curtain, opened the window, and peeped into the yard.

'Ay ay wot happenin boy Poon?' Ragbir asked.

Without answering, Poonwa slammed the window and went back on his bed. He listened. Basdai was in the kitchen cooking. Choonilal was talking to himself in the front room. His father was talking to himself about the Mission. This enraged Poonwa.

'Father, you don't have to talk to yourself about it!' he shouted. 'Today you have to sign those papers. Just remember that.'

Choonilal was shocked; he had no idea that he had been talking loud all the time. He thought that he had been talking to himself. Last night too he had been talking to himself, yet at times Basdai was able to hear him. A kind of nameless fright came over Choonilal. He had heard that talking to oneself was the first step toward insanity. Then the fright passed. He wanted to go insane just to spite Basdai. His mind wandered and he pictured himself running all over the village naked; Basdai was bawling and running him down. She had a pair of pants in her hand and she was crying and getting on. He felt good. But the fear came back again. Once he had gone to the madhouse in Spanish City to see a boy from Tola. The boy was locked up in a little room; the room was dirty; there was no bed; the boy was naked and the hair on his head was long and unkempt; his fingernails were untrimmed and bluish with dirt. When the wardman opened the door, Choonilal saw the mad child sitting on the floor and eating his own waste. Choonilal couldn't bear the pain of such a horrible recollection, so he called out, 'Ay Poon.'

'What the arse you want, Father?'

'Come nuh son and talk to you fadder. You is me chile boy.'

'What the arse you want to talk about?'

'O God Poon. I is you fadder boy. Have a little rispek for me nuh.'

'Respect my arse respect!' Poonwa shouted.

Choonilal lost his temper. He yelled, 'Poonwa!'

'Why are you bugging me, Father?'

And he: 'You modderass you! Lemme tell you someting boy. Lissen good! I ride you modder to make you! You didnt ride me modder to make me. Is I who ride you modder to make you. Always remember dat! If I didnt ride you modder you wouda never see de sun. And I ride she good too besides. Wen you de small you used to call me "fadder," now you does call me "Father." It look like English does flow from you ass. But all de book you read, Poonwa, and all dat education you have in you ass is notten. In dis same island man wid education have to eat dey shit! You is one man who have to catch you ass in dis world. From de time all you Indian boys get a little education in all you ass, all you does feel all you is God. But de days for Indians to see trobble comin soon.'

Poonwa said nothing.

Basdai had listened patiently. Now she left the kitchen and went into the front room. 'Wot de ass you makin so much noise for?'

Choonilal didn't answer.

'If you ass want to quarrel, I in de mood. De blasted chile want to go on de Mission, but you dont want him to go. But Choon, Poon have to go to Canada. I didnt care if I have to kill you ass!'

In those days gone by, Choonilal was a strong man when it came to quarrelling. This morning he began to quarrel out of sheer anxiety. The mortgage issue was killing him. He had toiled for thirty years under the burning sun; he couldn't just sign the mortgage. From the day Poonwa had talked about his Hindu Mission to Canada, from that day neither Choonilal nor Basdai had made a day's work on the sugar plantation. 'If we dont go out to work soon,' Choonilal said to Basdai, 'we go lost we badge.'

'Badge me ass badge!' she said. 'We not goin to work till you dont sign dat paper.'

Choonilal was exhausted; he remained on the bed and wept.

'You cryin like a woman!'

He said nothing.

Poonwa got up and came into the front room. 'Father, let us look at this thing in a reasonable way. It is not a mathematical problem. It doesn't call for analysis and data. Common sense alone is all we need.'

Basdai and Choonilal said nothing.

'History has shown that time and time again great ideas always had to face opposition.' He coughed a little and went on. 'When Galileo made his scientific discovery – '

'Who was Gatio?'

'Galileo was a scientist, Father.'

'You fadder stupid nuh ass yeh, he dont know one ting,' Basdai said.

Poonwa continued, 'Karl Marx had an idea, Father. That idea alone was able to transform Russian society.'

'Who was Kal Pax?' Choonilal asked.

'Dat simple ting you dont know?' Basdai asked her husband.

'Wot it is?' he asked her.

'I dont know, but Poon know,' she said.

Poonwa was growing impatient. Stamping his feet on the floor he said, 'Look at during the last war. Hitler and Mussolini were working with ideas. But their ideas were insane. My Hindu Mission to Canada is an original idea. History will remember me for it. All I need is the money, Father. The idea is unique.'

'I have notten to say, ' Choonilal said.

'In my Mission, all children will have to learn the Hindi alphabet. They will study only Indian History and Hindi Literature. They will have to dress like East Indians. Then I will build more schools and open Hindu temples for the white people to worship the Aryan gods. I will push hard. My Mission, so help me God, is to make white people good Hindus. I am going to make them feel that their culture is inferior, that the colour of their skin can justify their servitude. Within a few decades I will teach them to mimic Indian ways. Then I will let them go to exist without history. I will make East Indians buy up all their lands and claim all their beaches. Then I will drain all their national wealth and bring it to Tola. In this way I can make East Indians a superior people.'

Poonwa went on to talk about Hitler and Mussolini and their great determination and capacity for work. He was going to be another Hitler, he told them, but in the religious sense.

The ease with which Poonwa was drifting into the affairs of the larger world bothered Choonilal, not the way he was talking. English had always fascinated Choonilal and history was a thing that Choonilal had grown afraid of. Hitler didn't terrify him; Mussolini was the dangerous man. When Mussolini had invaded Ethiopia there had been a great deal of debate about the invasion in Carib Island. The Negroes were so excited that they bought newspapers by the dozens and wasted a great deal of time debating the matter in the cities. But soon the debate turned into an epidemic; the Negroes in the villages began to buy newspapers too. Then the Indians got the fever; they sided with the Negroes in the belief that the invasion was a threat to Carib Island. Literate and illiterate, it didn't matter, they all bought papers. And so the issue was debated in rum shops and by the roadside. Choonilal used to buy a newspaper and take part in passing judgment on the destiny of Europe; he didn't even know where Europe was, and Ethiopia was too far – he didn't really believe that Ethiopia existed, but it didn't matter; some of the journalists on the island didn't know where Ethiopia was. Choonilal couldn't read a word of English, but he used to sit in the rum shop and read the newspapers; and although all the news was printed in English it never bothered Choonilal.

Sook too had a taste for history in those days. He was a learned man; he had learnt to read English somehow. When there were no customers in the shop, Sook and Choonilal used to sit on wooden stools and talk about the invasion and the insecurity of the world. Sook used to read Choonilal's newspaper to Choonilal and explain to him the dilemmas of world politics. As the days went by, Choonilal had a feeling that he was strong enough to debate international affairs. With the newspaper in his hand, Choonilal argued as if he knew everything about the invasion of Ethiopia. One day a learned Negro man came into the rum shop to discuss the Ethiopian crisis with Sook. But Sook couldn't talk; there were customers in the shop. Choonilal felt that he was educated enough to discuss the crisis with the Negro. But Choonilal found himself in trouble right at the beginning; he had thought all along that Mussolini was a Negro, Ethiopia was a white country! He told the Negro that Mussolini was a blessed man: God was going to make him conquer his enemies. The Negro was a racist and a fanatic; pulling out a penknife, he ran up to Choonilal. When Choonilal saw the blade, he abandoned the debate and took the road. The Negro would have stabbed him, but Choonilal was a good runner.

Poonwa was still talking.

'Like you eh go stop talkin?'

'No Father.'

'But dis boy rude in truth yeh,' Choonilal said to Basdai.

'He have a right to be rude,' she said.

Poonwa ended abruptly and went back to his room.

'I dont cook food aready, Choon,' Basdai said.

'I not hungry.'

'Oright,' she said.

'Me ass "oright,"' Choonilal declared.

Basdai didn't say anything. She left the room and went back into the kitchen.

Choonilal closed his eyes; he needed sleep badly. Suddenly it dawned upon him that for the first time in many years he had neglected to defecate. Whispering something to the gods, he jumped out of bed. He felt giddy; for a moment the whole house was spinning. He changed his mind; he was not going to empty his bowels again; he was too weak to walk over to Ragbir's outhouse. He went back on the bed. But a sharp pain pulled at his guts. He ran out of the bedroom and hurried down the steps.

Ragbir was still helping Tailor to clean the pit. Ragbir said, 'Wot happen boy Choon? How you holdin you belly and runnin so?'

Choonilal wanted to say something, but the waste was too eager to come out of him. He glanced quickly at the road. There were too many cars going up and down; he didn't stand a chance to reach his neighbour's outhouse. Taking the track at the back of his house, he ran toward the sugarcane field.

'Like Choon have a tight shit,' Ragbir said.

'It look so to me,' Tailor declared.

Now the greater part of the work was over: all that remained was to scrub the floor of the latrine, nail back the seat, and attach the galvanized iron door.

'But Rag you is a modderass yeh,' Tailor said. 'You say you do come to help me clean de pit, but you didnt help one ass.'

'But I was wid you all de time man, Tail.'

'Yeh, but didnt help me man.'

Ragbir got mad. 'Tailor I never shit by Choonilal yet! I didnt have to clean no pit. Do everyting for youself. Oright.'

'Oright.'

Washing his hands and feet under Choonilal's pipe, Ragbir went into the kitchen to talk to Basdai. 'Ay ay Bass, wot happenin gal?' he asked as he sat on the cane bottomed chair.

'I still livin boy Rag.'

Pinching her hips, he said, 'Like you still have Julce in you yet Bass?' She didn't answer.

He decided to use the outhouse affair to get around to some more important business 'I de givin Tail a hand to clean de latrine gal,' he said. 'Just now Poon goin to Canada, you and Choon go have to have a farewell. Now de latrine not goin to smell no more.'

Although Basdai had had many affairs with Ragbir because he had the longest penis in Tola, she still felt that he was meddling too much in her household affairs. She said hotly, 'I is Poonwa modder. He goin to Canada on dat Mission by de hook or de crook. You and Choon and Sook cant stop him!'

This kind of talk made Ragbir think a little. He wondered for a moment whether Basdai was the same woman he had always known. Long time Choonilal used to argue and she used to remain quiet, but now the process had changed; she was doing the complaining and Choonilal was keeping his mouth shut. Ragbir laughed, 'You know gal Bass, you gettin me wrong. I de just tellin Choon dem tings because he is me friend. I still love you, gal.'

'Dont tell me dat!' she yelled. 'I know you too good Ragbir.'

Without saying another word, he patted her between the legs as he walked out of the house and went over by Sook.

It was about 1 p.m. Basdai and Tailor had been scrubbing the floor since Ragbir had left. As they scrubbed, Poonwa smoked a cigarette and watched them. All the rooms were clean; only the front room remained to be done. Basdai wanted to impress the lawyer and the priest with the cleanliness of the house.

'Let we go and do de front room now,' she said.

She walked in front with a broom. Poonwa followed her and Tailor trailed behind them with a bucket of water. When Basdai saw that the room was empty, she thought that her husband was in Sook's rum shop.

'Go and tell Choon to come from dat shop right now. And befo you go, bring dat rope you clean de latrine wid for me.'

'Oright,' he said, going downstairs to get the rope. When he came back, Basdai took the rope and, handing it to Poonwa, said: 'Put dis in you room, Poon.'

'Yes, Mother.'

As Poonwa left with the rope, Tailor left for Sook's shop. When he was inside, he asked, 'Choon by you?'

'Choon not by me,' the queer said.

Ragbir was sitting on one of the wooden stools and sipping a glass of rum. He asked, 'You mean Choon didnt come home yet? Like he shit out he guts and dead or wot?'

'I dont know,' Tailor said.

Rookmin panicked. She jumped up from her chair and said, 'Take care de man really dead yeh.'

Staring at them, Ragbir asked, 'All you ever hear shittin kill some-body?'

It was all right for them to talk and laugh. Sook was serious. He remembered the days he had shared with Choonilal; those were the days when Choonilal had lost his taste for women. It seemed to Sook in retrospect that those were the best days he ever had. He had been overwhelmed when he first encountered Choonilal. Their first affair began in daylight. Sook suggested that since it was Choonilal's first homosexual experience it was fitting to do it in a holy place, because his first affair with a man was always a sacred thing for him. Together they had walked through the backstreet until they came to the Anglican Church. The doors were closed, but a window was slightly open. Opening the window, they went inside the House of God. There was a large picture of Jesus hanging near the altar. Sook took down his pants and leaned over the altar, looking at Christ. Choonilal, wishing to make the best use of the affair, had ridden him smoothly. Suddenly the main door flew open; a robed priest walked in. Sook pulled up his pants and jumped over the window. Choonilal was too excited; he ran to the main door and knocked down the priest, then he took off naked through the backstreet.

'Wot you tinkin about?' Rookmin asked.

'Notten,' her husband said. 'I de just tinkin dat we shoud go and look for Choon.'

'Well all you go. I go stay in de shop,' Rookmin said.

Ragbir, Tailor, and Sook left the shop. Crossing the junction, they took the little track behind Choonilal's house. The sun was hot, but they walked until they came to the trace that separated the missing man's property from the sugarcane field. There was a general shock: Choonilal had emptied his bowels in the middle of the trace and had fallen asleep next to his waste. As the direct rays of the sun struck the excreta, it gave off a horrible smell. Sook spat and said, 'Choon is really a nasty modderass!'

Choonilal's head was about a foot away from the waste. Flies went with ease from the excreta to his opened mouth, and then to the excreta again. Ragbir said, 'Dis son of a bitch really nasty. I go never drink worta by he house again!'

Tailor wanted to wake up Choonilal right away; he didn't have the constitution to watch the freedom of the flies. But Ragbir had a good constitution. He said, 'Let Choon rest a little. We go wake him later.'

Remembering how long ago he and Choonilal used to hug and kiss, the queer shouted, 'Choonilal, you is a nasty bitch!'

With a slow deliberation Choonilal extracted himself from the dream. It was not an easy thing to do: his mouth had to open and close many times, thereby killing a few flies; once or twice he shook his head from side to side, an activity that brought his face closer and closer to the waste; once his right hand moved in a semi-circle above the crown of his droppings but by sheer chance the hand did not become unclean. Then he sat up and screamed, 'O God!!!'

'Wot happen Choon?' the queer asked.

Choonilal just lowered his head and maintained a heavy silence.

'De smell from de shit get him stupid,' Ragbir observed.

Basdai and Poonwa were sitting on the concrete steps. Basdai had on her best worried look. With her arms folded, she waited on the men who had gone in search of her husband. Numbness washed her body; her eyes felt calm but useless; her heartbeats became slower. This happened when she saw the men shouldering Choonilal home. 'Wot happen?'

'Notten gal Bass,' Ragbir said.

'How notten?'

'Well he de just smellin he own shit in de trace,' Sook reported.

Mrs Choonilal wore her worried look expertly. This made her son say, 'Don't take it on, Mother. Father is just kidding. He is trying his best to get away from the mortgage business. Well you know how he is.'

The hint drove the numbness away from her body. She whispered, 'I know dat, Poon.'

The men carried Choonilal and dropped him on his bed. They were willing to talk to Basdai; to talk and tell her how her husband had the courage to empty his bowels on the trace, how he had the nerve to sleep near his droppings, and how he had a number of flies for lunch. But with an iron firmness, Basdai ordered them out of her house; she said that she wanted to talk personally and confidentially with the ailing Choonilal.

Choonilal was glad when his wife left the room. Lying down on the bed, he gazed at the ceiling and thought about his life. He felt that the Aryan gods had abandoned him: from January to December he had prayed to them in the past; from Sunday to Sunday he had called their names and had told them to stand up for him in the time of need; through the sun and the rain he had laboured to build a resting place. The gods were ungrateful: he had prayed to them all his life; he used to pray to them very loud, begging them to help him in times of trouble. All his life he had been a good man; pennies and toil never spoilt him. In the past the gods had loved him. Sometimes when he had problems he used to sit by the Jandee pole and pray to them; sometimes during the rainy season when he had problems, he used to sit by the Jandee pole and pretend that there was no rain at all; and sometimes when the wind blew and the ripe chataignes fell from the tree, he used to pretend that there was no wind and there were no falling chataignes: he had done those things just for the gods. Unable to continue this trend of thought, he called, 'Ay Bass!'

'Oy!' she answered from the kitchen.

'You and Poon come here.'

Before they came into the room, Choonilal covered himself with the sheet properly. Wishing to make a good impression, he turned his head from side to side and groaned.

Basdai sat on the bed, but Poonwa remained standing.

'Like you sick Choon?'

'I sick too bad Bass.'

'Which part hurtin you?'

'All over me body hurtin, Bass. I feel dat I go dead.'

'You want to see a docta?'

'No.'

Then there was a short silence. Basdai winked at Poonwa and said, 'Like you fadder deadin Poon?'

Poonwa went mad with rage. 'Father, you are getting on like a cow's arse. You are not a man!'

'Watch you modderass mout boy!' the ailing man yelled

'Men like you, Father, shouldn't be allowed to live in the British Empire!'

'You tink dat is de British Empire who ride you modder to make you? Lemme tell you someting boy, I ride you modder to make you. And de British Empire modderass! Oright.'

Poonwa left the room.

Choonilal was sweating. Basdai took her orhni and wiped his bald head.

'Hush nuh,' Basdai said.

Choonilal blew his nose on the floor. He mopped it with an end of the bedspread. Then he scratched his balls and said, 'You hear how dat modderass cuss me?' Holding Basdai's right hand, he said, 'Lissen to me, Bass. We was livin togedder befo Poon de even born. Poon have no right to go to Canada. Wen we dead, he go get dis house and land. Why he want to go in dem cold contry for?'

She wanted to talk to Poonwa. 'I goin to make some coffee,' she said.

'Oright Bass,' he said affectionately.

Poonwa was in his room. The door was open. Basdai pushed her head in and waved at her son. Poonwa tiptoed out of his room and went into the kitchen with her. His mother opened a pipe hard; the water made a lot of noise. Then she started talking to him.

Satisfied with what his mother had said, Poonwa went back to his room. Pulling out his notebook, he scribbled:

### MEDITATIONS!
*As the universe unfolds, a woman's hole will become larger and larger. The angels will find a way to rape the fetus.*

Then he threw the notebook and the pencil under the bed. He thought of his school days. He had been enrolled in a secondary school in South City. It was a good school, the best for East Indians on the island. All the students were Hindus who had been converted to Christianity. The teachers were all followers of the blue-eyed Jew. The principal of the school didn't like Poonwa; without a reason, he was in the habit of taking Poonwa into the punishment room just to flog him on his naked bottom. Once the principal had kicked him on his spine. But he had graduated. Then he went job hunting. There was no room in the teaching service on the island for a Hindu boy. A few schools were good enough to interview him, but there was always the same story; he had to become a Christian in order to teach in one of the Canadian Mission Schools. It was too much. Giving up the idea of teaching, he decided to look for a good office work. He was faced with the same problems: office work was for Christians.

Suddenly Poonwa thought of the Canadian blond. He came down from the bed and, fetching the pencil and the black notebook, he wrote:

*CHRISTIANS ARE CRIMINALS!*

He wasn't satisfied. He screamed, 'Father!'

'Shut you ass!' Choonilal shouted from the next room.

Mad with rage, Poonwa ran out of his room. Standing in the doorway of the front room with trembling lips, he pulled out hair from his head.

As a bald-headed man this pained Choonilal. He shouted, 'Pull out you hair! Wen you ass get bald like me, den you go know de value of hair!'

Choonilal woke at the sound of a man's voice.

He was not sure whether it was a man's voice. Perhaps it was the sound of an evil spirit, he thought. He rubbed his chest. When he was fully awake, a strange kind of terror seized him; it was not the voice of a spirit or a god after all. Choonilal batted his eyes, and a cold sweat broke out on his forehead. He disliked what he saw. Closing his eyes tight, he tried to fall asleep again.

The lawyer, Poonwa's employer, was a fat black Madrassi Indian. His hair was trimmed very short and there were a few grey hairs on his head. His gold-rimmed spectacles pinched his nose; perhaps it was causing him pain, for now and then he rubbed his nose with the back of his hairy hands. In his dark suit he looked like an undertaker.

Pandit Puru was dressed in a clean Brahmin's gown, but he wasn't wearing the Pandit's topee. His face was clean-shaven, brown, and smooth. With his cowboy boots and the five diamond rings on his fingers, he looked like a gambler.

Basdai and Poonwa were in the room. They too were sitting on cane-bottom chairs and waiting on Choonilal.

Choonilal had been stubborn for the past two months. Now he was sorrowful.

'I know you wakin,' the priest said.

'I know dat too,' the lawyer added.

'Get up!' Basdai shouted.

He opened his eyes.

'We come to do business,' the priest said. 'You de sleepin long enuff. Now is time you sign de paper.'

Choonilal felt like vomiting. Escape was impossible. Fingering his thoughts a little, he said, 'Baba, today plenty ting gone wrong.'

'Tell we about dem,' the holy man said.

Choonilal had waited for hours just for an opportunity to talk about his illness. He said how earlier in the day he had felt a great need to defecate. He had been in the habit of using Ragbir's outhouse, but suddenly today he had felt that he had to defecate in the sugarcane field. But when he had reached the trace, he couldn't go inside the cane-field. Each time he tried to go inside the field, an evil spirit held his feet and pulled him back on the trace. When he found out that the spirit was pulling his feet all the time, he had sat on the trace and defecated.

'Dat is a sign,' the priest said. 'De gods dont like how you didnt sign de mortgage paper yet.'

Choonilal trembled.

The lawyer scratched his testicles and said, 'Let me give you some professional advice, Mister Choonilal. Never fool around with the Law and with God.'

Choonilal wanted to say that he was afraid of signing the paper more than he was afraid of the gods. But he said instead, 'I is a poor man.'

Pandit Puru shoved his right index finger up his nose; the finger turned and twisted as if he was dragging out some kind of expensive jewellery. Hauling it out gently the priest examined the green ball with care, then dropped it into his mouth and said, 'Tell we about you dream, Choon.'

He said that after he had emptied his bowels he tried to leave the trace and walk back home, but he couldn't. The evil spirit held his feet and kept him on the spot. Then he heard someone calling his name and he grew afraid. Somebody was trying to murder him, he thought. Suddenly a drowsiness had overpowered him. Falling asleep, he had dreamt his house; it turned into large bird and flew away. While he looked at his winged house in the dream, he felt a great pain in his belly.

'You de bawl out?' the priest asked.

'Yeh Baba.'

'Well you are an ass. You had no right to scream!' the lawyer shouted.

Choonilal continued. As soon as he had screamed in the dream, the house exploded; then the ruins turned into ten little creatures: they were demons with short black bodies and long red wings; they were not too ugly; their faces were like Poonwa's own. Each jumbie carried a wooden club. But as they approached him he had seen that the clubs were not really clubs; they were small sledge hammers. Some of the satanic forms walked into his mouth and tickled his tongue; others were content just to walk upon his lips. They were singing as they tormented him. Then they went mad; they pounded his testicles, and in the dream he saw his flesh scattering all over the place. Later the creatures devoured his scattered flesh; then they joined together and turned into his house again. A great wind sprang up; the house went into the air and turned into a vulture. The huge evil bird took out its penis and urinated on Choonilal.

'That is a bad dream,' the lawyer said.

'De gods vex wid you, Choon,' Pandit Puru declared.

And Basdai, 'Choon too harden.'

And Poonwa, 'Father is a rotten liar.'

'Kiss me ass!' Choonilal shouted.

The lawyer disliked the way things were proceeding: he had hoped all along that Choonilal had been worked over already by Basdai and Pandit Puru, but here was Choonilal with enough endurance to talk about absurd dreams. Scratching his head, the lawyer said, 'Now you listen to me, Mister Choonilal.'

'I lissenin.'

'You don't have to talk so rough!'

'I not talkin rough.'

'Did any of the urine go into your mouth?'

'Never,' Choonilal said. 'I de close me mout tight tight. Dat bird coudnt pee in me mout.'

'You are lyin!' the lawyer shouted.

Choonilal jumped up. Afraid to annoy the lawyer, he said, 'Yeh I de lyin. Some pee de gone inside me mout.'

'How de pee de taste?' the priest asked.

'It de taste like sand, Baba.'

'Any de gone in you eye?'

'Yeh Baba.'

'It de burn you eye?'

'Yeh Baba.'

'Dat is de sign dat you have to sign de mortgage papers.'

'I is a poor man, Baba.'

'Poor me ass poor!' the priest shouted.

'I cant sign de paper, sah?' Basdai asked the lawyer.

'If your husband was dead madam, you could have done it,' the lawyer said.

'I wish he de dead!' Basdai said.

'You modderass!' Choonilal screamed.

'Have some kiss-me-ass rispek for me, Choonilal!' Pandit Puru yelled.

'Father is lost forever,' Poonwa said apocalyptically.

'I didnt lost wen I de ridin you modder to make you?'

Pandit Puru decided to play his trump cards. Pulling out a small copy of the Bhagavad Gita, he recited in Hindi for Choonilal. Religion was Choonilal's greatest weakness; the priest knew it. Choonilal listened with tears rolling down his thin face. Then the priest stopped the recitation and began explaining the verses. He said that material things, things like houses, land, and money, were not important. Man's soul was the only important thing. The body is a product of matter; it could decay, but the soul was eternal. Then he handed the Holy Book to Choonilal. 'Swear on dat book dat you not goin to sign de mortgage. Swear on de Gita dat you not goin to send you son to teach Hinduism to white people.'

'I cant swear Baba,' he said.

'Sign de mortgage papers,' the priest said.

'I not signin none!' Choonilal shouted, as he flung the Gita away.

'De gods go make you blind! Dey goin to make worms fall from you mout! You goin to dead befo you time!' the priest yelled.

Choonilal was mad at himself; he had thrown away the Holy Book of the Hindus. He daydreamed that the gods had seen him when he flung away the book. About eight of them left their abodes in heaven and came screaming down to earth. Choonilal was running from them. They had fire in their eyes and they were swinging their hands madly. He ran out of his house and went over by Sook. He told Sook that the gods were mad at him; he had flung away the Gita and the gods were trying to kill him. Sook only laughed. He didn't believe. Then the gods reached by the shop. When Sook saw the gods he was terrified; he was a queer and the gods don't like homosexuals.

The daydream vanished.

With a trembling hand, Choonilal bent down and picked up the Gita. 'I sorry Baba,' he said. Pandit Puru didn't take the book. He just wore an expression of thought. Bursting into tears, Choonilal buried his head in his pillow. Poonwa ran from the room. Basdai screamed. Pandit Puru bawled out. The lawyer farted discreetly.

Taking up the pound of rope from under his bed, Poonwa ran through the hall with Basdai behind him. Poonwa got downstairs before her. Knotting the rope, slipping it around his neck, Poonwa climbed up the chataigne tree. Basdai stood under the tree bawling. Then the priest and the lawyer leaned out of the window and yelled.

'Wot happen Baba?' Choonilal asked, lifting his head from the pillow.

'Your son is about to hang himself!' the lawyer shouted.

Jumping out of bed, Choonilal gazed out of his window. He saw Poonwa with the rope around his neck. 'O God! O God! Poon ... '

'Not 'O God! O God!" the priest shouted. 'Sign de mortgage papers befo de boy kill heself!'

'I go sign it Baba! I go sign it,' Choonilal moaned.

The lawyer leaned out of the window again, laughed a little with Poonwa, and said, 'You father is going to sign those papers, boy.'

Now that the priest had Choonilal where he wanted him, he didn't intend to waste time. Leaning over the window he said to Poonwa,

'Stay on dat tree wid de rope around you neck. Dont come down till you fadder sign de paper.'

The priest winked at the lawyer to get out the papers. Pulling them out, the lawyer handed Choonilal a pen and said, 'Sign here quick!'

'I cant write.'

The lawyer signed for him.

'Come fast, Basdai!' the priest yelled.

She too couldn't sign her name; the lawyer signed for her also.

'Get witnesses!' the lawyer shouted. 'Fast.'

Standing on the verandah, Basdai called Sook, Rookmin, Ragbir, and Tailor from the shop. Tailor and Rookmin signed as witnesses; Sook and Ragbir wanted no part of the matter.

Leaning over the window again, Pandit Puru said, 'Come down now, Poon. Choon business in order.'

❖

It was late, and the Madrassi lawyer and the chauffeur hadn't returned from Spanish City as yet. The priest was waiting on the car because he couldn't walk the half-mile back to his house. He was sitting on the couch next to Choonilal and smoking continuously. Choonilal sat like a dead man; his face was pale, and his eyeballs were watery. He had a red cloth wrapped around his bald head. Ragbir and Sook rested on two cane-bottomed chairs as they spoke to the priest and Choonilal. Basdai and Rookmin were in the kitchen cooking food.

Poonwa was happy. He sat on his bed and talked to Tailor; on the floor, Tailor listened. Poonwa described Europe and the United States. Tailor's intellectual horizons didn't extend beyond canefields and villages; he was glad to welcome the enlightenment. When Poonwa said, 'There are over one hundred million queers in Europe and America,' Tailor said. 'You sure?'

'I am certain.'

'You mean white people does bull too?'

'Certainly.'

'I de tink dat only Indians and Creole does bull. Wot you tellin me dere boy Poon? White people in Carib Island does do like dey does shit ice cream, now you tellin me dey too does bull. Me God, I never hear dat befo boy Poon. You mean dat you de know dat all de time and you never tell me, boy Poon.'

'You never asked me.'

'Dat is true,' Tailor admitted.

Tailor envied Poonwa's education for the first time in his life.

Poonwa shifted a little on the bed. 'All the Greek philosophers were queers.'

'I dont care one ass about de Greeks.'

'What do you think about Christianity?'

'It look like a good religion to me.'

'There is where you are wrong. In principle it is good. But it is a dangerous religion.'

'How?'

'Christianity is nothing but a slogan for wars and aggression,' Poonwa expounded. 'Christianity enslaved the Negro and raped all the primitive peoples.'

Confused, Tailor said, 'But boy Poon, to me tinkin was Christian people who stop Creole from pullin cart.'

'You are an arse!' Poonwa said hotly.

Poonwa was not really mad with Tailor. While he was talking about Christianity, the white woman he had kept as a prisoner in his mind came back to torment him. Mentally Poonwa whipped her and locked her back into his brain cells. Then he switched the topic. 'Do you know that in the civilized world there are more sexual crimes committed than in the backward countries?'

Popping out his eyes, his listener said, 'You dont mean dat!'

Quoting a book he had borrowed from the Hindu priest, Poonwa said that he knew of cases in which civilized women had seduced their sons, and men their daughters, and he mentioned the fact that some lonely housewives were in the habit of copulating with broom and mop handles; the more adventurous ones took to lorry gear shifts.

Teenage girls in America had perfected the art of masturbation as they sat on bicycle saddles.

Tailor butted in with, 'Yeh man Poon. But dem ting does happen in Carib Island too. It had a woman in Rajput Road who used to do it wid a donkey. Anodder gal in Gran Couva used to do it wid a snake. A woman in Bhagi Tola used to do it wid plantains, yeh. Dem ting does happen on dis island man.'

Suddenly it dawned upon Poonwa that he had made a mistake. Tailor was a specialist in village affairs. One day he had shown Poonwa his little notebook in which he kept names and addresses; he had lived in almost every village on the island. There were pages of notes about the lives of the various people he had encountered. Again, Tailor was an experienced man: he had seduced Sook and had brought whores to Karan Settlement too often. Poonwa envied his listener for the first time in his life.

The village tailor laughed strangely.

'What are you laughing at?'

'About de night Phyllis de runnin you down.'

This was hardly the proper time for Tailor to mention the incident. It had happened more than a year ago. One night Tailor had brought Phyllis to Karan Settlement. That night Basdai and Choonilal had gone out; Poonwa was alone upstairs. Tailor had called him. When he went downstairs, he got a shock. Phyllis was standing naked behind one of the concrete pillars. Tailor had whistled, and the whore ran, and grabbing Poonwa, she had dragged him inside Tailor's little room. Poonwa had never had a woman; and when he saw the hairs between her legs he had screamed and run back upstairs.

Poonwa switched the conversation to the climate of North America. 'Do you know that ice falls from the sky in Canada?'

Tailor was bowled over.

Poonwa named the four seasons, but he based his lecture on winter; he didn't talk about rainfall, sunlight, and clouds; Tailor had seen these. Poonwa knew all about Canada from his days at the Mission School. He spoke about blizzards, those wicked winds that were in the habit of destroying barns and killing off livestock; about the ice that fell from the sky and froze a few people to death each year; about the nakedness of the trees and the havoc of regenerating death. 'What do you think about that?'

The bleakness of winter numbed Tailor; he didn't answer.

Taking advantage of Tailor's helplessness, Poonwa switched to History. He talked about the red Indians who had been living for thousands of years in North America, just living with nature and worshipping the land. Then came the white man with his Bible and guns and a paper that had been given to him by some blue-eyed king; the paper said that the king owned the land; the Indians were trespassers. Then there was war. There was death in the land. Then the white man drove his railways as spikes across the earth. Suddenly there was smoke and activity; two mighty and God-fearing nations came into being. The Indians were rounded up and placed on reservations.

'With the paper of ownership in a drawer and the Bible under his head,' Poonwa said solemnly, 'the white man sips whisky as he dreams of peace.'

Tailor faked a cough. 'You coud talk good, Poon. But talkin is not all you know. Dat night wen Phyllis de want to give you a little bit, you de run like a bitch.'

Then Tailor laughed hard and Poonwa smiled coldly.

'All you come and talk dis side, nuh. Come nuh Poon!' the priest called.

Poonwa and Tailor came into the hall. Ragbir and Sook got up from their chairs and sat on the floor. Poonwa sat on Sook's chair, but Tailor said, 'I go siddown on de floor, yeh. Me eh great like Poonwa yet. Just now wen Poon go Canada, he woudnt know Tail again, nuh.'

Fingering his stained blue towel with one hand and scratching his beard with the other, Ragbir said, 'Baba.'

'Yeh,' Pandit Puru answered.

'Just now wen Poon go Canada, he go forget all of we yeh. You know wen dese Indians go over and come back to dis island, dey does do like dey get white. And anodder ting Baba. Wen Poon go over and he get a little bite of a white woman, he go forget Karan Settlement clean, yeh.'

Scratching his balls thoughtfully and peering at Poonwa, the priest said, 'All woman is de sameting, son. God make all women wid hole. As a priest, lemme say dis. Wen Poon go to Canada, he cant stay in he room and watch he totey all de time. He have to move heself. He must ride a little woman now and den. But he have to have he head on. He must never forget to tink about de Mission.'

Wishing to make use of the enlightenment he had received so generously from Poonwa, Tailor said, 'But I hear in dem cold contries, women does do it wid dogs.'

Choonilal had been sitting quietly on the couch with the red cloth around his head, but when he began to hear about the lechery of white women, he threw the cloth away. 'I wish Poonwa couda dead,' he said. 'I wish some woman couda bite out he stones in Canada!'

'Have some rispek, Choon,' the Pandit said.

Picking up the red cloth from the ground, Choonilal wrapped his bald head again. Choonilal was thin, but he had a large bald head; there were wrinkles under his chin and dark circles around his eyes. He had only a few teeth in his mouth, but he had never seen a dentist all his life. Whenever he had a toothache, Basdai used to take a pair of pliers, drag him into the bedroom and extract the infected tooth. Once she had almost broken his jawbone.

Choonilal groaned.

'Wot happen Choon?' the priest asked.

'Me teet hurtin me Baba.'

Basdai came out of the kitchen with coffee cups on a small wooden tray. She passed it around; everybody took coffee except Choonilal. Then she said, 'Baba.'

'Yeh,' he answered.

'Give Poonwa some advice eh. Tell him dat wen he go over, to write me. Tell him not to married no Jawman woman. You hear Baba.'

Everyone in the house knew about the case of the German woman. An East Indian boy from Caribville had gone to England to study medicine. When he was qualified, he had married a German woman and brought her to Carib Island. But when he brought her there he found out that Carib Island was different from England. There were clubs in

Spanish City in which coloured people were not allowed. Even with his medical degree, the East Indian couldn't enter the white clubs, but his German wife was accepted. It didn't take her long to learn from the local whites that coloured people were inferior to her, and she began to live a bawdy life. Developing a hate for all natives in the West Indies, she began to mingle only with whites. The Indian doctor murdered her and threw her body into the Gulf of Tola. He was executed.

'Wot de ass you tellin him!' Choonilal screamed. 'You make me mortgage me modderass house and land! I work to make dis all me life ... '

'I woudnt rob you house and land Choon,' the priest said.

'But you run raffle and send you kiss-me-ass son and dem to India! You collect money to build temple, and you didnt even build de temple.'

'Wot me son and dem do, I not responsible for dat!' the priest shouted.

And Basdai: 'Ay Choon! Watch you ass! Watch it. If you talk up you ass, it goin to have trobble here tonight!'

'You goin to make me beg in me old days, woman,' he said.

'I dont know why you dont dead!' Basdai shouted.

Choonilal groaned and all his teeth began to ache. Basdai hadn't said that to him very often. There were times when he used to beat her and run her all over the village, but she never wished him to be dead. Bursting into tears, Choonilal threatened to drown himself in the outhouse.

Ragbir said: 'Woman is trobble yeh. Dat is de reason why I never keep a wife.'

'But you like to ride woman?' Basdai asked.

'Yeh.'

'Maybe dem Americans and dem used to bull you in de base. You, huh!'

'Dat is any of you business, woman?'

'Sure it is me business!' Basdai said. 'A man like you shouda shame Ragbir. You does play Choon friend. But you woudnt tell Choon how much time you ride me.'

Choonilal cried out, 'All you modderass, wen all you dead all you goin to born back as worms!'

Then Rookmin ran out of the kitchen. She said, 'Baba read someting about God, nuh. Or give Poonwa some advice. Bass, you come back in de kitchen. Come and let we talk gal.'

Basdai and Rookmin went back into the kitchen and sat down. 'You gal Bass, dat is a wrong ting you say just now. Not everyting you must talk.'

'Dat Ragbir just goin too far. He was de man who was behine Choon all de time. He was tellin Choon not to sign dat mortgage paper. You hear. And dont tink Sook backward eidder. Dese mens, dey just like woman, I tell you gal Rook. Choon wouda done sign dat paper two monts ago. Now so Poonwa de reach Canada and forget. From de day Choon start to shit in Ragbir latrine, from dat day de trobble start.'

Rookmin believed this. For months there had been no quarrelling in Choonilal's house. Even the night Phyllis had knocked down the wall of the outhouse, there was only a little noise. But from the very morning that Choonilal had emptied his bowels in Ragbir's pit, the row began. Wishing to get Basdai in a better mood, Rookmin said, 'I remember someting gal.'

'Wot?'

'I remember de time you and Choon de stick up like go dogs.'

Basdai laughed. Her whole body shook. 'Dat was someting eh gal, Rook.' Basdai drank some more coffee and then laughed again.

'Wot you laffin at gal?'

'I laffin about … about de time … you and de watchman de doin it in de road.'

Rookmin laughed. That had happened a long time ago. About twenty years ago there was a watchman in Indian Estate. It was believed by the people that he had a long totey, even longer than Ragbir's. Though the rumour was started by Ragbir, it became popular among the village women. Ragbir used to collect money from the women and collect money from the watchman as well. Then the women used to leave their husbands in bed at night and go into the road to meet the man. Something was wrong; the village women never cared to talk about their encounter with the blessed watchman. One day Ragbir went into the rum shop. Sook was not there; he had gone to Spanish City. Ragbir had his opportunity at last. He told Rookmin about the watchman with the long penis. She felt that Ragbir was lying; he had to swear on the Christian Bible to convince her. She still didn't believe. Then Ragbir left her alone. But as some time passed the idea of meeting the watchman became an obsession with Rookmin. Ragbir knew the psychology of village women well; each time that Rookmin tried to talk to him about the man, he used to say, 'Look Rook, dat man very busy. He have hundreds of women waitin on he. You tink he have time wid you, nuh.' As Rookmin heard this she thought that the watchman must have had something great between his legs. One day she gave Ragbir some of Sook's money. She begged him to get the watchman to come and meet her that night. Putting the money in his pocket, Ragbir went and spoke to the watchman. That night Ragbir brought the man to Karan Settlement. He flung a pebble on Sook's house, a sign for Rookmin to come out. When she came out, Ragbir went and sat under Choonilal's chataigne tree. On the middle of the road, the lecherous watchman had seduced her. Wishing to make a good impression on the shopkeeper's wife, the watchman told her to go down on her hands and her knees. She refused. The man begged her. She went down on her hands and knees. Then there was a bawling; the lecherous man drove it up the wrong hole. Rookmin screamed and screamed. Sook ran out of the house. With a torchlight in his hand he saw his wife's position and he laughed out loud. Choonilal and Basdai ran out on the road also; then Ragbir came too. Rookmin was still getting on, but the men were about to kill themselves laughing. Suddenly Basdai grabbed the man's testicles and squeezed. He bawled out and withdrew his organ; Sook gasped in amazement. Wishing to get away from the maniac, Rookmin ran toward her house, leaving a yellow line in her wake.

Pandit Puru said, 'Wot de ass all you womens laffin for? All you come here. I goin to read someting from the Ramayana.'

She and Rookmin came out of the kitchen. They sat on the floor near the priest.

With a slowness common to those of the priestly caste, Pandit Puru fished out an old copy of the Ramayana that he had kept hidden somewhere in the lower part of his gown. The sacred copy was old; the covers were threatening to fall apart. He opened the book. Scanning a few pages, he closed it and pursed his lips.

No words were necessary. Basdai got up and went into her bedroom. Opening the wooden bureau, she took out ten dollars from a brown leather wallet. Handing the money to the priest, she said, 'Take dis Baba.'

Pandit Puru grabbed the crisp bill and stuck it in the vest pocket of his gown. Then he opened the Ramayana.

Ragbir said to Choonilal, 'Boy Choon better you come a Pandit yeh. Pandit does talk about heaven. But dey well know how to tief on de earth!'

Pandit Puru stamped the floorboards with his cowboy boots. He said forcefully that Choonilal's attitude to the Aryan gods and Hindu rituals would get him in trouble after death. He said that the gods were merciful, but that Choonilal was dooming himself; the gods didn't like people who wouldn't give generously to priests. For his attitude alone, Choonilal would be trapped into the unending cycle of birth and death. Pulling out the ten-dollar bill from his breast pocket and flinging it at Choonilal, he said, 'Keep you kiss-me-ass money!'

Basdai was grateful to the priest because he had tolerated Choonilal's stupidity and sudden rages quite well. Jumping up like a horse, she kicked Choonilal on his bald head as she shouted, 'Shut you ass now!' Then she bent down and took up the money from the floor. She handed it to the holy man with, 'Take it Baba.'

He took it.

'When are you going to deliver the money, Father?' Poonwa asked the priest.

Not wishing to talk about the embarrassing question of money, Pandit Puru said, 'Lemme give you some advice Poon. Never forget dat you fadder is Choon. Didnt care if you catch you ass, never forget dat you modder is Bass. Stay away from Rag and Tail, even if you have to make a jail. Wen you reach on Canadian soil, never forget … to change you oil.'

And Tailor: 'Baby, you is a kiss-me-ass poet!'

And Ragbir: 'Shakspoor couda never write poetry like dat!'

And Poonwa: 'Not "Shakspoor" you arse! Shakespeare!'

'Shakespeare de born in India,' Tailor said.

'Dat is korek,' the priest said.

'Shakespeare was an Englishman!' Poonwa shouted.

'Shakespeare was an Indian from India. He de born in dat same India, you hear dat. He dead in India too,' Pandit Puru said.

Choonilal, wishing to make up to the priest, said, 'Baba is korek. Shakspoor de born in India.'

The priest smiled at Choonilal; he returned the favour.

Wishing to get back to the money issue, Poonwa asked, 'When are you going to have the money ready, Father?'

'We go see about dat tomorrow.'

'Thank you, Father!' Poonwa said.

Even Choonilal looked happier and healthier.

'You tink dat Poonwa go get through in dat mission, Baba?' Choonilal asked.

'Yeh! De odder night I see Poon travellin in a acroplane. I de see Lord Krishna sittin next to him on de whole journey. Wen he reach to Canada, Krishna come outta de plane wid him. Den Lord Krishna put flowers on top Poonwa head. Dat mean dat de mission go succeed.'

'Poonwa have no right to go on no kiss-me-ass Mission!' Ragbir said. 'He shoud get a woman and settle down in Karan Settlement.'

'Why didn't you take a wife and settle down?' Poonwa asked.

Ragbir was bowled over.

'Poonwa not goin to study woman in Canada,' Basdai said 'He goin to see about dat Mission.'

And Pandit Puru, with his practical vision, saw an opening. Licking his scabby lips, he said, 'Yeh Bass, you korek. But lemme tell you one ting. Dem big contry is not like Carib Island. In dem big contry women does wear pants and men does wear pants. It hard to tell which is de man and which is de woman. But de boy go have to have a little ting now and den. He go have to change he oil some time.' Turning to Poonwa, he continued, 'Son, I is a man of God. Lemme give you an advice. Wen you go over, work hard on de Mission. Oright. But we is big people. Try and change you oil. Dat is important. Take dis as you feelosofee in life: If a woman lie down for you, ride she! If a man bend over for you, bull him! Never spear de rod!'

Sook giggled.

If that remark had been made by Sook or Ragbir in the presence of Poonwa, the Choonilals would have waged a war against the corruptor. But Pandit Puru was a holy man. So without speaking at all, Basdai and Choonilal agreed whole-heartedly with the advice. But the priest saw that although they had consented, the Choonilals were embarrassed. Not wishing to find out why Choonilal and Basdai were staring at each other almost distractedly, the priest said, 'I go read now. All you be quiet.'

Tailor yawned; he was sleepy. But he couldn't leave now. Poonwa would be away soon; then he would be able to live in Poonwa's room, seduce Basdai, use the washroom upstairs, and beat up Choonilal. He sat quietly.

Ragbir didn't believe in Pandit Puru, but he had a great deal of love for the Aryan gods. Of late he had been constantly bothered by his dreams. At times his past came back to haunt him. And while he was sitting on the floor fingering his favourite towel, the thought of death passed through his mind. Afraid to contemplate it, he said, 'Read someting holy, Baba.'

Pandit Puru read a passage from the Holy Book. Sita, the beautiful wife of the Hindu God Rama, was stolen from him by Rawan, the evil king of Lanka. Rowan was prevented from ravishing Sita, because the monkey God Hanuman was a friend of Rama; he couldn't allow his friend's wife to be seduced by such a wicked king.

'How Hanuman de born Baba?' Tailor asked.

According to the priest, there was an answer to the whole mystery. Hanuman's mother was a very beautiful woman. She was clean too; every morning she used to go and bathe in the sacred river, then she used to sit naked and dry herself in the sun. One day Pawan the God of the Wind was passing. He looked. He saw the naked woman asleep in the sunlight with her legs thrown wide apart. The temptation was great; he raped her.

Ragbir said, 'I cant see how he coud ride de woman widdout wakin she up?'

The priest asked, 'You coud see wind Rag?'

'I coud break wind, but I cant see it,' Ragbir replied mournfully.

'Well de sameting Rag,' the mystic said. 'De God of de Wind invisible. Dat is de reason why wen he ride de woman, coudnt feel notten.'

'But he had to leggo some wortta inside she to make chile.'

'Dat is true,' the priest said, 'but de wortta was invisible wortta.'

'Then it was vapour,' Poonwa said.

'Korek.'

'But Baba,' Basdai said.

'Yeh beti?'

'How Hanuman de born a monkey?'

The explanation came quickly: Hanuman was not a real monkey; he just had an ugly mouth, a prank played upon him by the higher gods. He had been born an ordinary child with a pretty face. But when he was only a few months old, he called upon his father Pawan. When the God of the Wind came, He found out that His bastard son wanted to go to the moon and the sun. Hanuman was greedy; he decided to eat the sun. There was a goddess guarding the sun from any invasion, she went mad when she saw the half-earthly bastard trying to swallow the light of the sky. She struck him with a club; that was responsible for his ugly look in later life.

Ragbir laughed and said, 'I dont see anyting so great in dat.'

Pandit Puru shouted, 'Hanuman was greater dan Jesus! Hanuman de born in a palace. Jesus de born in a blasted cowpen!'

Poonwa liked this very much. He said, 'The place for Christians are cowpens, Baba. My mission will show the Christians the beauty of Hinduism. Americans are Christians and Russians are Christians, yet they hate each other's guts. My mission will teach the white world compassion. They have lost it!'

'You coud read Hindi?' Sook asked.

'No,' Poonwa replied.

'Den how de ass you goin to teach Christians about Hinduism?' Ragbir asked.

'I would like to ask you something.'

'Ask me,' Ragbir said, eyeing him seriously.

'The Christians who first came to this island on the Canadian Mission to preach Christianity, did they know Hindi?'

'No.'

'If the first missionaries only spoke English and they were able to convert the Hindus, then it will be easier for me to teach them about Hinduism in their own language.'

'But dey had schools, and books and ting,' Ragbir said.

Poonwa said that it was nothing; he would build a school in Canada too. Instead of having one punishment room like the Canadian Mission School had in Tolaville, he was going to have about five such rooms. Through flogging and teaching he would pound Hinduism into them. Then he would teach them to deny their culture; he would make them wear Hindu garments. Then he would get merchants from Carib Island to tie up their trade and drain their national resources into the West Indies. But now and then he would give them a little money as aid also; and he wouldn't give them the money just like that; he would make them crawl and beg for it. Then he would teach them that white is ugly and evil; only black and brown are good …

Poonwa's voice got louder and louder, until the bald-headed chauffeur called, 'Ay Baba!'

'Come.'

The lawyer and the chauffeur came into the house. Choonilal said to the lawyer, 'You bring de money?'

'I done tell you you gettin de money tomorrow!' Pandit Puru shouted.

The lawyer and the chauffeur sat in the hall. Smiling, the Madrassi lawyer asked Poonwa, 'Have you made contact to open the Hindu Mission School in Canada yet? These things should be handled expertly. Especially in those white countries.'

The lawyer was an experienced man; he had studied Law in England.

'I do not think it is necessary to plan,' Poonwa said. 'When the Canadian Missionaries came to Carib Island, they didn't come with blueprints; they just came. Then they built schools and began to convert the children. They didn't teach them anything about their own culture.'

'But where will you get the money to open the school?'

'When I reach there I will think about that.'

Choonilal was impressed. His fascination for the English Language sprang up again. He realized that for the past two months he had been hard-headed; Poonwa was not a fool.

'You have to be very careful on such a mission,' the lawyer said. He had studied Law in Oxford but spoke English with a West Indian accent.

'Actually, nothing is impossible,' Poonwa said. Although he hadn't been to England, he spoke English with an Oxford accent.

As Poonwa continued to talk, the white school mistress broke loose from his brain cells. He felt her running all over him. He screamed, 'The Hindu Mission to Canada will succeed!'

The lawyer trembled a little, and said, 'What is the use of the Hindu Mission to Canada? I was educated in a Canadian Mission School in South City. I am proud of it.'

'Are you blind?' Poonwa asked rhetorically. 'Christianity broke the spirit of the Indians and the spirit of the Negroes as well. Today on this island the young Indian boys are drinking rum and fighting and killing each other. You just have to read the newspapers to know that. There is a reason for this. They have no culture. They are lost! They are worse off than the Negroes. Today the Negroes are searching for their culture, and they will find it! But the Indians are lost. Indian culture had not been completely broken by the Indenture System. Today the Indians, instead of making use of their cultural heritage, they are ridiculing it, and making a mockery of it. Soon they will become a people without identity.'

The priest winked at the lawyer, a sign for him to keep his mouth shut.

Choonilal felt that it was his turn to say something to his son. With his arms folded he said, 'Well Poon, I de ride you modder to make you. Up to now I does ride you modder now and den, but I gettin old now, son. Remember wen you reach Canada dat you fadder mortgage dis property to send you dere son. Try and send a little money to help me pay back Baba. Never forget boy dat you pee and shit fust touch dis earth in Karan Settlement. Didnt care where you livin in dis world, never forget home.'

Bursting into tears, he extended his arms to embrace his only son. But as his father approached him, Poonwa ran out of the house. At this, Choonilal cried louder, so Pandit Puru comforted him by speaking of the Mission to Canada.

After listening to the priest, Choonilal, still weeping, sat down.

As the priest was trying to calm Choonilal, Sook sneaked out of the house to look for Poonwa. He found him standing on the middle of the junction.

'Wot happenin, boy Poon?'

'I am just trying to enjoy the night.'

'Like you tinkin about Choonilal and dem?'

'As a matter of fact, I am thinking of my Mission.'

'It is a nice night yeh, Poon,' Sook said in a sweet, womanish voice. 'It is full of beauty.'

'You go remember me wen you go over, Poon?'

'I'll remember every one of you, because you are all a part of my dream.'

Without warning, Sook grabbed Poonwa's crotch and held fast. Poonwa jumped aside and said, 'Try and behave yourself man.'

This didn't discourage the queer. He kept his hand where it was and began to massage.

Poonwa tried to unlock his fingers, but Sook was determined not to let go. Sook said, 'I go give you one hundred dollars if you bull me.'

'Are you certain?' Poonwa asked.

'I swear to God.'

'I can't do it.'

Being a sentimental man, Sook broke into tears without any warning. 'It is a nice night yeh,' he sobbed. 'And since tonight you first time, we go do it in de Christian Church.'

On any other night Poonwa would have allowed the queer to weep his heart out, but suddenly, seeing it as an opportunity to get even with the Christian blond and the blue-eyed Jew, he nodded.

'All right,' he said. 'I'll bull you for free.'

'You dont want de hundred?!'

'No. This is my farewell gift.'

Sook shook his head and opened the eastern door of his shop. Uncapping a stout, he handed it to Poonwa.

'Drink dat fust,' he said. 'It make you iron stand like a lion.'

Pandit Puru was still giving advice to the Choonilals.

Rookmin looked up and found that Sook was missing. Remembering that Poonwa had left the house too, she slipped out unobserved. She saw the half-opened door of the shop. She could not hear anything, but when she saw the empty stout bottle on the counter she called out, 'O God! O God!!!'

When Rookmin screamed, the people in Choonilal's house ran out to see what had happened. They ran straight into the shop; Rookmin was still bawling and getting on.

'Wot happen Rook?' Pandit Puru asked, with deep concern in his voice.

Ripping off her dress and slipping out of her panties, Rookmin stood in the nude with her legs wide apart. Then pointing to her hairs, she said to the people, 'All you watch good! Watch de nice fat ting I have. Sook does leave dis fat ting to go and take man. Tell me if dis world have any reason in it?'

'Never doubt dat gal,' the Hindu priest said, kneeling in solemn reverence. 'Dis world do have reason in it.'

Then, gazing between her legs, he licked his lips. 'You ting really fat and juicy Rook!'

**Harold Sonny Ladoo** was born in Trinidad and Tobago in 1945 and immigrated to Toronto, Canada, with his wife and son in 1968. He is the author of *No Pain Like This Body* and his second novel, *Yesterdays*, was published posthumously in 1974.

Typeset in Albertina and Brice.

Printed at the Coach House on bpNichol Lane in Toronto, Ontario, on Rolland paper, which was manufactured in Saint-Jérôme, Quebec. This book was printed with vegetable-based ink on a 1973 Heidelberg KORD offset litho press. Its pages were folded on a Baumfolder, gathered by hand, bound on a Sulby Auto-Minabinda, and trimmed on a Polar single-knife cutter.

Coach House is located in Toronto, which is on the traditional territory of many nations, including the Mississaugas of the Credit, the Anishnabeg, the Chippewa, the Haudenosaunee, and the Wendat peoples, and is now home to many diverse First Nations, Inuit, and Métis peoples. We acknowledge that Toronto is covered by Treaty 13 with the Mississaugas of the Credit. We are grateful to live and work on this land.


Cover design by Crystal Sikma, cover art by Andil Gosine and Kelly
    Sinnpah Mary
Interior design by Crystal Sikma
Author photo by Graeme Gibson

Coach House Books
80 bpNichol Lane
Toronto ON M5S 3J4
Canada

mail@chbooks.com
www.chbooks.com